A JACK CHRISTIE ADVENTURE

DAY OF
DELIVERANCE

JOHNNY O'BRIEN

templar

A TEMPLAR BOOK

First published in the UK in 2010 by Templar Publishing
This softback edition published in 2011 by Templar Publishing,
an imprint of The Templar Company Limited,
The Granary, North Street, Dorking, Surrey, RH4 1DN, UK
www.templarco.co.uk

Copyright © 2010 by Johnny O'Brien
Illustration copyright © 2010 by Ian Andrew and Nick Spender
First softback edition
All rights reserved
ISBN 978-1-84877-097-3
Cover design: butterworthdesign.com
Editorial by Anne Finnis, Helen Greathead, Ruth Martin and Rachel Williams
Picture research by Caroline Reeves

Printed and bound in the UK by Thomson Litho Ltd., East Kilbride, Glasgow
The right of Johnny O'Brien to be identified as the author of this work has
been asserted by him in accordance with the Copyright, Designs
and Patents Act 1988.

PICTURE CREDITS

©TopFoto pp. 10–11 (map);
p.25 (Christopher Marlowe);
p.60 (execution of Mary, Queen of Scots);
p.150 (Spanish Tragedy artwork);

p.195 (Spanish Armada map);
decorative borders throughout.
© Bridgeman Art Library
p.22 (Elizabeth I, Armada Portrait)

For Sally, Tom, Peter and Anna – J. O'B.

The Year: 1587

The Place: London

The Mission: To save Elizabeth I – England's Glorious Queen

Catapulted back in time to Tudor England, Jack Christie and his friend Angus must foil a plot to assassinate Elizabeth I.

Joined in their adventure by playwright Christopher Marlowe and a young William Shakespeare, the boys must prevent a dramatic change in the course of history, and keep their heads in the face of deadly intrigue.

Day of Deliverance
A JACK CHRISTIE ADVENTURE

CAST OF MAIN CHARACTERS

Jack Christie – Our hero

Angus Jud – Jack's loyal friend

Carole Christie – Jack's mother

Professor Tom Christie – Jack's father

Dr Pendelshape – The slightly unhinged history teacher

Counsellor Inchquin – Leader of VIGIL

The Rector – Headmaster of Soonhope High and
VIGIL second-in-command

Secondary Characters

Edward Alleyn – An actor

Miss Beattie – English and Drama teacher and nuclear physicist

Belstaff – Games teacher and VIGIL security

Elizabeth I – Queen of England

The Fanshawe Players – Harry Fanshawe's failed group of travelling actors

Harry Fanshawe – An actor

Philip Henslowe – A businessman & theatrical impresario

The Henslowe Players – Philip Henslowe's professional acting troupe

Theo Joplin – VIGIL historian

Thomas Kyd – A playwright

Mary, Queen of Scots – Queen of Scotland

Christopher Marlowe – A playwright

Monk – An actor

Jim de Raillar – Bike shop owner and VIGIL analyst

William Shakespeare – A playwright

Tony and Gordon – School janitors and VIGIL minders

Trinculo – An actor

Professor Gino Turinelli – Italian bistro owner and Professor

Sir Francis Walsingham – Principal Secretary of State and Privy Councillor

Whitsun and Gift – Revisionist agents

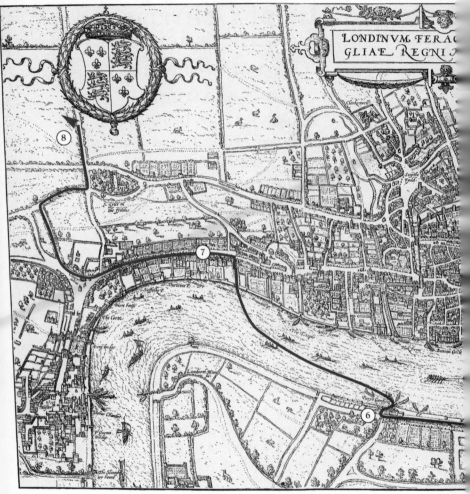

JACK'S FIRST TRIP

1. The Cross Keys, Gracechurch St
2. London Bridge
3. Heads on Sticks, London Bridge (south)
4. The Rose, Liberty of Southwark

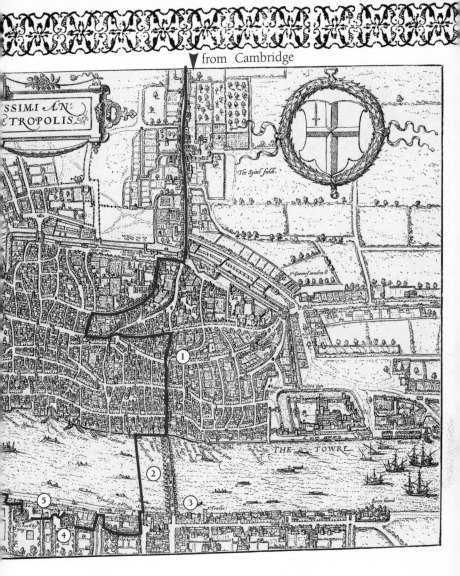

from Cambridge

TO LONDON

Contents

Jack's Adventures So Far...

It has been six months since Jack and Angus made the mind-boggling discovery that their school, Soonhope High, is a front for a team of scientists who control the most powerful technology ever conceived by man: the technology of time travel. At the heart of this technology is a machine called the Taurus, and Jack's dad, Professor Christie, was part of the team that originally designed it. Jack hasn't seen his father since he was six, when the scientists who formed the Taurus had a serious disagreement and Christie was forced into exile, leaving Jack and his wife, Carole, behind.

Christie's plan was to use the technology to make changes to the past – stopping major wars, for example – that would make today's world a better place. He attracted some passionate and brilliant supporters, including Dr Pendelshape who, until last year, was Jack's History teacher. Pendelshape and Christie, together with their small band of followers, who call themselves the 'Revisionists', developed sophisticated computer simulations to model interventions in the past that could benefit mankind. Their former colleagues, on the other hand, continue to believe that changing events in the past, however well meant, would be dangerous and have unforeseen consequences. Once Professor Christie was out of the way, they formed a group called 'VIGIL' to ensure that the Taurus was kept secret – but in working order should it ever be needed.

Jack and Angus had become embroiled when, unknown to VIGIL, Christie created a *second* Taurus and proceeded to try to stop the event that triggered the First World War – the assassination of the Archduke Ferdinand, in Sarajevo, June, 1914. Pendelshape acted as Christie's partner, continuing to teach at Soonhope High and leading VIGIL to believe that he was loyal to them. Meanwhile, Jack and Angus were used as pawns in a battle between the two camps. Jack's loyalties had been torn. In the end, having witnessed first hand the dangers of time travel and intervening in the past, Jack decided that the right course of action was to side with VIGIL.

Since then, there has been a stalemate, with neither side able to make a move against the other. Not knowing the whereabouts of Christie's base, VIGIL can do nothing about the second Taurus. Christie, on the other hand, will not use his Taurus while Jack is under the guard of VIGIL. The members of VIGIL know that Christie will do nothing while there might be a threat to his son, in retribution for any action the Revisionists take. But Christie does not know that Jack's loyalties are now with VIGIL, and Carole Christie is also firmly inside the VIGIL camp. The atmosphere at VIGIL is tense. Although their security is highly sophisticated, they wonder what the Revisionists' next move will be...

A Poisoned Sword

Jack thrust the rapier forward. Angus jumped back, but this time he was not quick enough. The blade pierced his flesh and an ominous red patch appeared on his white shirt. Angus glanced down at the wound and looked back at his opponent with an expression of rage on his face. A frisson of excitement rippled through the crowd. The contest was proving far better than they had imagined. Jack was exhilarated – one final blow and it would all be over.

His confidence was short-lived. The strike had found its mark but he'd also momentarily lost his balance and Angus came back with a violent counter-thrust. His blade flashed through the air and caught Jack in the ribs. There was a gasp from the crowd. The foil was so sharp that Jack scarcely felt it. But in only a few seconds his own blade grew heavy in his hand and his breathing quickened. Sensing his chance, Angus darted forward once more, his sword aimed at Jack's chest again. This time Jack spotted the move and swayed to one side. Angus's forward momentum presented Jack with an opportunity. He grabbed his opponent by the arm and heaved him onwards, while simultaneously thrusting out his leg. Angus tripped and spun through the air landing with a crunching thud, his sword spinning from his hand. Jack pounced onto him and they became locked in a deadly struggle. But he should have known better than to take on Angus in a wrestling match. Angus was much too strong and soon he had Jack pinned on his back beneath him. He grasped Jack's sword hand and banged it hard on the ground until Jack relinquished his grip. Angus lowered his face towards Jack's and sneered.

"You will die."

Jack was nailed to the ground. He was wounded and he had no weapon. Angus's massive bulk was pressing down on him. But it wasn't over yet. He gritted his teeth, and with a super-human effort jerked his knee upwards into Angus's crotch. Angus wailed in pain and Jack seized the moment to wriggle free. Snatching up a sword, he wheeled round. The sword felt different – heavier and unbalanced – but it didn't matter now. Angus jumped back to his feet and grabbed the other sword and the two of them circled round and round, panting at each other like wounded animals. The crowd jeered. Jack's remaining energy was melting away – he knew he only had seconds left. There was blood all over the floor and Angus slipped. He was only distracted for a split second but it was enough. Jack leaped forward to land a second, fatal blow. Angus screamed as blood from a second wound spurted from his chest. He dropped to one knee, and looked up at Jack. It was an unexpected expression – almost apologetic,

"The poison... I am killed with my own treachery..." He stammered.

Jack glanced down at the sword that dangled loosely from his hand – and suddenly he understood. He had snatched up his opponent's sword, which Angus must have dipped in poison before the contest. Jack had already been injured with the same sword, which meant that, in less than a minute, both of them would be dead.

But there was still time to see to unfinished business. Jack knew what he had to do.

Clutching his chest to stem the bleeding, he staggered across to where his uncle sat cowering behind the long banqueting table. The food and drink was laid out – still untouched. Jack mounted the table and fixed his eyes menacingly on his uncle who sank back into his chair, shaking. There was to be no mercy and Jack did not hesitate. He thrust the sword into his uncle's heart.

Words, Words, Words

Miss Beattie scurried onto the stage, "Well done, everyone! Lights!"

There was a spontaneous round of applause from the cast and crew. Nothing was being left to chance. The week before, Miss Beattie had even arranged for a special fight choreographer to come in and help them with the sword fight between Hamlet and Laertes in the last scene. It was all perfectly safe, of course, and the flashing swords reassuringly blunt, but there was always tension in the air during the famous scene and everyone stopped what they were doing to watch. And today, with Angus a reluctant and unrehearsed stand-in for the real Laertes who was off sick, anything might have happened.

"That's all coming together quite well." Miss Beattie said, pleased with their progress. "Only two weeks to go now..."

Jack looked down at Tommy McGough from his position high up on the table. Tommy was playing Claudius, Hamlet's uncle, and he nervously opened one eye.

"Did I survive?"

"Looks like it," Jack said. "Don't know how you get away with it. Every rehearsal I somehow manage to miss."

"Dangerous business this Shakespeare stuff..."

Angus bounded over from centre stage, flushed with excitement after the sword fight.

"That was awesome..."

"Told you..."

Angus's shirt was almost completely red as Miss Beattie removed the pouch of stage blood from underneath it.

Day of Deliverance

"What a mess," the English teacher fussed.

Angus grinned, "I thought I would go for Hamlet meets Terminator... Everyone likes a bit of blood, don't they, Miss?"

Without looking up, she replied, "Actually, you're right. When they performed these plays in the old days they wouldn't have skimped on the blood... they'd have used real goat's blood probably. The audiences loved gore. There's even a story of actors using a real musket. In one production it went off and someone in the audience had his head blown off by mistake."

Miss Beattie was always coming out with stuff like this. It was one reason why Drama was so popular at school – and successful. The whole town of Soonhope would probably turn up for the end-of-term performance of *Hamlet*.

"Is that true, Miss?"

"Apparently. They just dragged the body out. Next day they were on again. I doubt they used the musket again, though health and safety wasn't top priority in the sixteenth century..."

"I could get into that," Angus said.

Jack elbowed him. "See – told you it was worth coming."

"Well – the fighting was good fun, but I couldn't stand Shakespeare for too long – you know, all those... words."

Miss Beattie looked up at Angus with a steely eye, her good humour evaporating. At nearly six foot, Angus towered over her, but somehow, the expression on her face made him shrink.

"You've done it now..." Jack murmured, casting a sidelong glance at Tommy, who grimaced in return.

"Words!" Miss Beattie rolled the 'R' in her strong East Scots brogue. "WORRRDS!" She repeated it – louder – and it came from her lips like a dart from a blowpipe. "Is that all you have to say on the matter – WORRRDS?"

Everyone around the stage stopped what they were doing and turned to look at Miss Beattie. For all her boundless enthusiasm, she was also prone to dramatic changes in mood. As a result, Angus was about to receive what was popularly termed by the pupils of Soonhope High School as 'a Beattie Beating'. It was never pleasant.

"But, Miss..." Angus bravely tried to stand his ground, but it was too late. It was as if he had inadvertently triggered a small thermonuclear device.

"I'll tell you this – laddie – not any old words... nearly one million words in forty plays and more than one hundred and fifty four sonnets and poems... and not just any old plays and sonnets, but the most sublime writing the world has ever read – even after four hundred years. Words? Shakespeare invented them. Lots of them... like: *critical, frugal, dwindle, extract, zany, leapfrog, vast, hereditary, excellent, eventful, lonely...* and phrases... new phrases like: *vanish into thin air, brave new world, fool's paradise, sea change, sorry sight, in a pickle, budge an inch, cold comfort, flesh and blood, foul play, baited breath, cruel to be kind, fair play, green-eyed monster...*" She paused only to take a deep breath. Then she was off again. "These are WORDS and phrases that have been used so much they have become clichés... they are words and phrases that I use – God help us – even *you* use them, my lad – Shakespeare was the world's greatest writer. He helped define the world's richest language – the English language – *your* language. He gave us the very tools to think and feel. He gave us the *essence of humanity...* do you get it? Do you understand? So please don't talk to me about WORRRDS!"

There was stunned silence around the stage as everyone wondered if there might be more – whether this was to be a tactical nuclear strike – or the full-blown strategic version that would take out the whole of Soonhope. Thankfully, the colour in Miss Beattie's cheeks normalised from a deep purple to its more usual pink. Nevertheless, Angus continued to stare at a spot on the end of one of his shoes for a full ten seconds before finally mumbling, "Yes, Miss. Sorry, Miss."

Miss Beattie gave a final sigh of indignation and said, "That's all right, Mr Jud." She looked around and clapped her hands. "Now everyone – let's get this lot cleared up. It's nearly four o'clock."

But something that Miss Beattie had said stuck in Jack's mind and as he and Tommy put away the props, his curiosity overcame his fear of re-lighting the blue touch paper.

The auburn-headed Queen Elizabeth I in 'the Armada Portrait'

"Sorry, Miss – did you say a *million* words? I mean written by one man – Shakespeare?"

"Yes, Jack, I think that's about right."

"But that sounds like an awful lot for one man to write..."

"It is. There are lots of theories – most of them rubbish – that he did not actually write his material, but that others did. Shakespeare lived during the 'English Renaissance' – it was a boom time for plays and playwrights and art and artists generally. More than fifty candidates have been suggested as the 'real' Shakespeare – people like Christopher Marlowe."

"Who?"

Miss Beattie was overseeing the flow of props back into the store cupboard, giving orders as she worked. "No, Tommy, put the swords into the sword trolley *properly*, or they'll get damaged." She looked back at Jack. "Sorry, Jack – what was that?"

"Marlowe – was he like Shakespeare, then?"

"He influenced Shakespeare, but he died in 1593 before Shakespeare's career had really got going. He was only twenty-nine... it was murder. He was a spy."

"A writer and a spy?"

"Yes, maybe even a double agent. I know it sounds odd, but there were quite a few writers who were at the time – not Shakespeare, though. They often studied at Oxford or Cambridge; the universities were hotbeds of radicalism."

"What do you mean by radicalism?"

She sighed. "You're insatiable, Jack." She turned to lock the store cupboard and then looked at him sympathetically. "Look – we don't really have time to go into the whole of sixteenth-century politics right now... but next lesson maybe we'll do it in more detail." She thought to herself for a minute. "Tell you what, come over here..." She scurried over to a pile of bags at the side of the stage and pulled out a large book.

"There you go, that should get you started." She handed the tome over to Jack. It was entitled, simply, *Elizabeth I*. On the front cover was the famous *Armada Portrait* of the auburn-headed queen in an elaborately decorated dress covered in jewels with one hand draped over a globe and pointing to Virginia in the Americas, England's first colony in the New World. Behind the queen, the Spanish Armada could be seen, sailing to its doom.

"Knowing you, Jack, you should be able to finish that off in a couple of hours. It's all there. And it's not just about Shakespeare and Marlowe you know. This was a period of deep religious conflict – between Catholics and Protestants – a struggle for the very soul of man. And this religious conflict was intertwined with the political struggles between states. Spain was the global superpower and England was a backwater by comparison. But when England defeated the Spanish Armada, that all started to change. Otherwise, we might be living in a Catholic country today and speaking Spanish – and so might most of the world. We would probably be having tapas for school dinners." Miss Beattie stopped. "There I go again... prattling away..." She tapped the book. "Anyway, I'll leave it with you."

Jack leafed through the first few pages.

"Who's that?" He pointed to a picture of a confident young man in what he took to be flashy Elizabethan clothes.

"That's him – Marlowe," said Miss Beattie, "Only portrait ever made of him – he was just twenty-one and dressed up to the nines."

"What does that mean?" Jack pointed to some Latin words beneath the picture.

Miss Beattie laughed. "'What feeds me destroys me.' Just about sums Marlowe up. How shall I put it – he liked to live life on the edge."

Jack didn't really understand what she meant but he was already leafing through the rest of the book. There were pictures of ships: great Spanish galleons stuffed with treasure from the New World; terrifying fire ships let loose by the English on the anchored Spanish fleet off Calais; *The Revenge* demasted in the Azores, where, in a fit of macho bravado, Sir Richard Grenville took on twelve great Spanish galleons single-handed, only to die. There were extraordinarily beautiful new buildings, soaring edifices of glass and stone – a far cry from the brutal castles of the Middle Ages. Then there were the people: kings and queens, princes, players and poets... One chapter was called 'The English Renaissance' – and it seemed to live up to its

Christopher Marlowe:

'What feeds me destroys me'

billing. As Jack leafed through the volume, he noticed a small frame at the bottom of one of the pages. The caption read, 'Elizabethan Troupe'. It was a colour plate of a group of actors in various costumes. There was one dressed as a court jester and next to him, in stark contrast, another dressed as a priest or, more likely, a monk. There was a third who looked slightly more important – a country gentleman with a fine cloak and a neat, pointed beard.

"Head in a book again?" Angus leaned over Jack's shoulder.

It looked like nearly everyone else had gone. "Do you want to get something at Gino's?"

Jack snapped the book shut.

"Why not?" He stuffed it in his bag.

"Well, stop reading that rubbish and let's go."

Gino's

Jack sat pillion on Angus's motorbike. He was nervous. Usually trips on the back of Angus's bike did not go well. Angus was seventeen now and had passed his bike test. His old 125cc Husqvarna two-stroke had been left in one of the sheep sheds at his place up at Rachan and he had taken to riding one of the farm's more powerful four-stroke Yamaha 250Fs. When he could afford the petrol, he took the bike to school – avoiding the one-hour journey on the bus that picked its way painfully round the hamlets of the upper Soonhope valley.

Angus turned back the throttle and the engine wailed; he dropped the clutch and they set off. Thankfully, Angus omitted the wheelie he usually performed just to frighten Jack. Soon they reached the bridge over the river, which was quite low from a dry spring. The big Presbyterian church at the head of the High Street loomed ahead of them and Jack remembered what Miss Beattie had been saying about the 'struggle for the soul of man'. Even in Soonhope, with fewer than two thousand inhabitants, he knew of at least five churches, all of different denominations. It occurred to Jack that he hadn't actually been inside any of them, and he wasn't sure how many of the local population had either.

The High Street was busy but Angus managed to squeeze the bike right in front of Gino's and, as they went in, the welcoming smell of warm coffee and ice cream wafted over them. Gino was manning the espresso machine while Francesca, his daughter, polished glasses grumpily. Gino was as jolly as ever.

"What can I get you, lads?"

"Hi, Gino." Angus looked up at the endless menu of drinks and snacks pinned to a board above the counter. But he already knew what he wanted. "I'll have the double Gino-chino, extra shot, full fat, with caramel and extra cream... and don't forget the cherry." He looked over at Francesca and winked provocatively, adding in a deep voice, "Shaken, not stirred."

Francesca rolled her eyes and tutted loudly. Gino glanced up. "You have no chance there, the Turinelli family's outta your league."

Angus shrugged. "Oh well – I'll have four chip butties as well, please, Gino."

"Cutting back?" Jack asked.

"Not exactly. We're playing Melrose the day after tomorrow – last game of the season. If we win, we're champions. Need to bulk up."

"And Jack, my friend, what are you having?"

"Thanks, Gino. I'll go for a Gino-chino as well – but without the bells and whistles and make it just one chip butty."

"Coming right up. Take a seat, boys."

Gino had recently tried to convert his popular Italian bistro into an American diner – he had even got himself a juke box (which didn't work). It had been a brave attempt, but somehow it all looked a bit out of place in the traditional High Street of Soonhope. Jack and Angus settled into one of the booths and soon, in hushed tones, they were discussing their favourite subject.

"Do you think we did the right thing?"

It was Angus's first question. Jack thought for a moment and came up with his usual answer.

"Yes – we did the right thing. I'm sure of it. Dad and Pendelshape created brilliant computer simulations to test out the changes they wanted to make in history, but you could never be certain that by going back in time you might not do something that would have unforeseen consequences for the future. That's the risk. That's the whole reason VIGIL was set up. And that's why we had to side with them."

"Suppose. Pity though."

"Why?"

"Well... I know going back to 1914... Well, it was dangerous and stuff, and a lot of bad things happened..."

"Yes, Angus," Jack said slowly, making sure the point sank in, "that's why nobody wants to be doing it again. Time travel and especially using the Taurus to make changes to history... it's a bad idea. Remember your great grandfather Ludwig in the trenches? If that bayonet had been a few inches to the right, he might have died and, you wouldn't be here."

"I know, but..." Angus grinned. "You've got to admit, it was pretty cool."

Jack shook his head. "Sometimes I wonder about you. We can say that, sitting here now. But it didn't feel cool to me at the time. We were lucky to get away with our lives. Meddling in time is definitely to be avoided. VIGIL – and their leaders – the Rector, Councillor Inchquin – all of them – they're trying to do the right thing. Dad and Pendelshape, the Revisionists, for all their brains and good intentions, are just plain wrong. We're on the side of VIGIL now."

Angus shrugged.

Gino ambled over to their booth. "Two Gino-chinos, one chip butty for you and... four for you."

"Great Gino. Thanks a lot."

Jack looked at Angus's plate, "You're not seriously going to eat all that are you?"

"I don't really want to... I'm doing it more out of a sense of duty to the team," Angus replied regretfully, as if he were making some terrible sacrifice. He opened one of the butties and poured salt, vinegar and ketchup onto the chips inside before quickly re-sealing them within the bread. Then he took a large bite and the contents leaked out from each side.

"Gross."

"Actually, very tasty," Angus replied, his mouth full. It didn't stop him from continuing their conversation.

"But what about your dad? Don't you feel bad about him? If VIGIL ever gets hold of him, they'll do him for sure."

Angus was never one for subtlety and Jack grimaced. "Thanks for reminding me." There was an awkward silence and then Jack shrugged. "I try not to think about it." He swallowed. "And, I don't know, maybe one day there will be a way... a way that VIGIL and Dad can be reconciled." He looked down at his plate. "Maybe then Mum and Dad could even get back together."

Angus swallowed and took a swig of his Gino-chino. "Sorry Jackster – didn't mean to..." He shrugged. "Well – you know."

"It's all right. Anyway – we're fully signed-up members of VIGIL now. Don't forget what that means."

Angus wiped his mouth and his eyes lit up. "How could I forget?"

Jack remembered the VIGIL inauguration ceremony that he and Angus had taken part in after their return from Sarajevo. As things settled down, they learned that VIGIL's aim was not only to be ready to counteract any Revisionist attempts to meddle in history, but also to identify and train promising students and enrol them into VIGIL. This recruitment was one reason for secreting the Taurus complex and VIGIL headquarters in an ordinary school: it was easy to identify potential candidates. In this way, VIGIL would ensure the continuation of its cause from one generation to the next and ensure the future safety of mankind as well. This was critical, particularly while the Revisionist threat was still alive. Jack and Angus's experiences in 1914 had made them instant VIGIL veterans and obvious candidates for enrolment.

Jack's mobile went off and he pulled it from his pocket. "Text from Mum probably, wondering where I am..."

Angus returned to his chip butty.

Jack peered at the screen. "Don't recognise that number..." He opened the message. "Funny..." Jack's brow furrowed. "What do you reckon to this?"

"To what?"

Jack read out the text. "Jack – meet at old lookout. Very urgent. Come now."

"What can that mean?"

"You've got an admirer – finally."

"Hilarious."

"The old lookout – that's the fire tower, isn't it? You know, top of Glentress... we used to go up there on the bike."

"Yeah – but who's this from? There's no name."

Angus grinned mischievously. "Only one way to find out."

"But I can't do that without alerting VIGIL... I've got this stupid tracker on my ankle – remember?" Jack pulled up one leg of his trousers a little to show Angus the discrete wireless tracker that ensured VIGIL always knew his whereabouts. Jack was a valuable asset to VIGIL, and the tracker was just one of the ways they made sure he was properly protected. Most of the time he forgot about it, but sometimes it made him frustrated and even angry about the responsibility that rested on his shoulders.

"Oh yeah." Angus thought for a moment and then a twinkle came to his eye. "On the other hand, it might be a laugh to see how quickly they send in air support when they know you've gone AWOL. It's good to keep them on their toes."

Jack was not sure. "I don't know, Angus."

"Come on, Jack, who dares wins and all that." He nodded at Jack's butty and stood up. "Scoff that and let's go and find out who your mystery girlfriend is."

The Tower

In a moment they were back on Angus's bike heading out of town and towards the forest. The Forestry Commission owned large tracts of land above Soonhope, and had populated it with pine and spruce plantations that spread for many kilometres across the hills. Soon they were powering up one of the forest tracks, a plume of dust rising from the back tyre. At intervals there were fire warning signs with a picture of a red flame and lists of 'DON'TS' beneath – 'DON'T' do this and 'DON'T' do that. It was as if they'd been put there by VIGIL themselves. But you would need more than that to deter Angus. He worked his way up and down the gears as they ascended steadily. At one point the forest track swept round to the right and a steep path rose through the thick woodlands at an angle from the bend.

Angus pulled up and shouted through his helmet. "Hold on – I'm going to take a short cut."

Before Jack had time to object, Angus had re-selected first gear and the bike shot up the narrow path. All Jack could do was hang on. After a while, the steep path levelled off and they picked up speed, the densely packed conifers whizzing past on each side of the narrow track.

Suddenly, a shape appeared in front of them, right in the middle of the path. It was a man, just standing there, looking at the oncoming bike as if caught in a trance. Angus hit the front brake and then the rear a split second later. He twisted the handlebars to avoid the man and, as he did so, both tyres lost their grip on the loose track surface. In an instant, the bike, Jack and Angus were horizontal and sliding along the ground. The man leaped free, moments before impact, and the boys slid to a halt in the tall grass on the verge. Jack's heart was pounding. His leg hurt from where the bike had pressed down on it as they scraped along the track. Thankfully nothing seemed to be broken. Angus was first to his feet.

"What the...?"

Jack groaned and pulled himself into a sitting position. He looked up and immediately wished he hadn't. He felt nauseous.

The man looked at them from the side of the track. They had slid past him by a good twenty metres. He was, maybe, mid forties, slim and fit-looking and wore jeans, hiking boots and a grey fleece jacket. He had not shaved for a few days and his yellow hair was ruffled.

"What the hell are you doing – trying to get us all killed?" Angus bellowed.

The man did not reply. It was as if he were weighing up something in his mind. Then, still saying nothing, he turned and melted back into the thick, dark woodland.

Angus was apoplectic. "What? He's just run off!"

Jack pulled himself to his feet and dusted himself down. He could see the grazing on his leg through rips in his jeans.

"You okay?" Angus said. "Can't believe that guy!"

"We probably shouldn't be on this track anyway." Jack looked down at the bike, still lying on its side. "Will it start?"

Angus hauled the machine up, inspecting the scrapes to the petrol tank and chrome.

"What a mess. If I ever see that bloke again..."

He straddled the bike and tried the engine. It fired immediately.

"Thank God for that."

"What now?"

"Well we might as well finish what we came up here to do." Angus looked at Jack's pale face. "If you're still up for it."

"I'll survive." Jack mounted the passenger seat gingerly and Angus set off, this time at a more sedate pace.

After a while, they left the cover of the dark green canopy and were released onto the open heather moorland above the treeline, where they re-joined the main track. Apart from the mystery hill walker they had nearly hit on the way up, there was no one around and the fire tower loomed into view as they crested a final ridge.

Angus cut the engine and the air became still. They took off their helmets and walked towards the tower. Jack moved with a slight limp but Angus seemed to show no ill effects from coming off the bike. Sometimes it seemed like he was indestructible.

"Can't see anyone here at all. No sign of your mystery admirer."

Jack shrugged. "Weird. Shall we go up?"

They clambered up the wooden ladder to the lookout cabin.

Angus knocked on the rough wooden door. "Hello! Anyone at home?"

There was silence, except for a light spring breeze which teased the top of the trees in the distance.

"Nothing. Come on, let's check it out."

The door opened into a crude wooden room with panoramic views of the surrounding forest and hills. It was like being in a small boat in a big green ocean. Far below you could see the river meandering its way down the valley, shining like a silver ribbon in the late afternoon sun. In the middle of the cabin was a rough, three-dimensional model, a sort of topographical map of the surrounding area. It showed the hills, the main plantations, tracks, streams, the river, each peak, each village and the positions of the other fire towers. The whole world was suddenly defined in detail across a square metre of plastic and modelling paint. From this lofty position you could see how the fire wardens would have a sense of control... of watchful power.

"Nothing here. Certainly no clue as to your mystery texter."

Jack peered into the one adjoining room. It was a bedroom – but it was more the size of a large cupboard.

"Hey – looks like there's been someone sleeping here."

In the room, there was a sleeping bag, a gas burner and a couple of books.

"One of the wardens?"

"Bit early in the year."

"And I'm not sure they'd be reading these."

Jack picked up a couple of books that had been left behind. One was entitled *Principles of Quantum Mechanics*. It looked old, and was by someone called Paul Dirac. The other book was a complete works of William Shakespeare. It was open at one page and the reader had circled an extract in pencil. Jack peered down at the book.

"That's funny – this guy's been reading *Hamlet*."

"Please no, I've had enough of *Hamlet* for one day." Angus looked around furtively. "Beattie's probably got this place wired, just to check I don't say anything dodgy."

Jack read the circled extract from the book:

"Let us go in together;
And still your fingers on your lips, I pray.
The time is out of joint; O cursed spite,
That ever I was born to set it right!"

"Sorry, Jackster that sounds like complete gobbledegook... as per usual."

Jack smiled. "It's actually one of my speeches from *Hamlet*."

"I suppose you're going to tell me what it means and make me feel stupid?"

"Of course. From what Beattie says, Hamlet's basically saying that things in Denmark, which he calls 'the time', are all messed up because of what his uncle, King Claudius, has done – killing Hamlet's father and marrying his mother. Hamlet's thinking about what he has to do to put it right... and he's kind of worried and also resentful that he's the one who's got to sort it out. Do you understand?"

"No."

Jack rolled his eyes.

"All I can say is it's a bit weird that this guy's up here and maybe we shouldn't hang around too long. He might come back. I don't want to bump into some hobo living here all on his own who reads Shakespeare and Maths books for fun..."

"So who sent the text – do you think it was the guy who's been hanging out here?"

"It's all too creepy. I think we should go."

They turned to leave. As they did so, they noticed an envelope

pinned to the inside of the wooden cabin door. Jack's heart leaped
when he saw what was written on it. It was in an italic scrawl and read
simply: 'Jack Christie'.

Jack pulled the envelope down and ripped it open. Inside was a
letter:

Jack,

I had hoped to be able to meet you in person and have time for a
proper talk. However, I fear that VIGIL may soon learn of my location
and therefore I have had to leave in haste. This is a sad time for me.
You already know about my exile from my former colleagues in VIGIL.
It grieves me that, because of this, I have not been able to see you or
your mother over the past nine years. But now, I also find myself in
disagreement with my friend Pendelshape and the Revisionist team. We
were once so unanimous in our opposition to VIGIL. But now...

Some months ago we started work on a new timeline simulation –
one that aims to bring about great good for humanity. However,
I could not accept further development of this simulation before
I knew that you could be safely isolated from VIGIL and brought over
to our side. Pendelshape and my Revisionist colleagues have become
frustrated by my attitude, to say the least. We have argued and now,
fearing their retribution, I have left them. Furthermore, with your
safety in mind, I have, as of today, taken the unprecedented step of
warning VIGIL of what I know of Pendelshape's plans. I now find
myself alone in the world – a fugitive.

I never wanted to put you in this position or to expose you to all
you have experienced. However, I live in hope that we can one day meet
and that you will join me in my mission.

Dad

Jack stared at the letter in stunned silence. It all came together in
his head – the strange books in the tower... the man on the track...

"Your dad... he's been *here*?" Angus said, incredulously.

"Yeah. And I think that was the guy we nearly ran down. I thought I sort of vaguely recognised him. He was running away..."

"From what?"

"From just about everyone, I think."

Suddenly, in the distance they heard a faint mechanical whirring. Jack and Angus peered out from the front of the fire tower in the direction of the noise.

"And probably from that thing..."

The whirring rapidly crescendoed into a pounding *whup, whup, whup* as, below them, a large helicopter skimmed the tops of the trees and headed up towards the fire tower. In seconds, the helicopter was hovering right above them. The noise was deafening and it shook the wooden structure of the tower to its foundations. The pilot circled once before descending, the thrashing rotor blades throwing up a maelstrom of dust and debris. Finally, it touched down on a flat patch of ground near the tower and the pilot cut the engine. Jack and Angus opened the door of the cabin. Speeding along the forest track they could see three Land Rovers driving in convoy. As the noise from the helicopter engine subsided and the Land Rovers pulled up near the tower, Jack could hear loud barking from the back of the vehicles. Dogs.

Pendelshape Panic

Two figures stepped down from the helicopter. They crouched low to avoid the rotor blades that were still spinning at a dizzying speed. One was a tall man in his forties with fine features. He had an air of distinction and authority about him. It was Councillor Inchquin. The Councillor was Chairman of VIGIL and oversaw all its operations. Next to him was another tall figure – slimmer than Inchquin with a bald head fringed with thinning wisps of grey hair. By day he was Soonhope High's headmaster – the Rector – and he was still wearing his trademark black gown. The Rector was VIGIL's second in command.

Mr Belstaff and Mr Johnstone, the school games teachers, who also formed part of VIGIL's security and response team, stepped from the leading Land Rover. All members of VIGIL had day jobs that belied their second life as key members of the VIGIL network. The four men converged on Jack and Angus who stood nervously at the bottom of the fire tower.

"Is he in there?" the Rector said, aggression in his voice.

"He's gone." Jack replied.

"Damn." Inchquin hissed. "No sign at all?"

"He left this letter." Jack handed the letter they had found inside to the Rector who scanned it quickly.

"Well – it confirms the message we received earlier," the Rector said. "You saw nothing else?"

Jack was torn. The dogs cooped up in the Land Rovers were in a frenzy. Was Jack really going to admit that he and Angus had nearly run down someone they thought to be his father, only for VIGIL to release a pack of hounds on him in some brutal manhunt?

The thought had not even crossed Angus's mind. "We think we

might have seen him." He nodded down the hill. "But I don't think you'll find him now."

Inchquin looked at Jack sympathetically. "Sorry, Jack – we have to try. He's too important just to let go." He turned towards Belstaff and Johnstone. "Take the other men and the dogs – see if you can track him down. He might not have got far. Hurry."

"What's going on, Sir, how did you know he would be here?" Jack said, "… and… what does the letter from Dad *mean?*"

"We intercepted your mobile message. And then the tracker alarm indicated you were exiting the Soonhope safe zone. Sorry, Jack – you know we can't take any chances." The Rector waved the letter in the air. "And this letter basically means trouble. We will explain back at HQ." He nodded at the helicopter. "You need to come with us. We have very little time."

"Hey – what about my bike?" Angus said.

"The men will take care of it. I can assure you we have much more important business to attend to. Now, let's go."

The sun was in the west and hanging low in the sky. Angus and Jack peered from the helicopter as it swooped in above Soonhope High's extensive playing fields. Jack was pretty sure no one had arrived at school in quite such style before. Pity there was nobody there to see it. They had a bird's-eye view of the austere Victorian school building which sat in secluded grounds some way out of the town. Until ten years ago it had been empty. It was then re-developed by an endowment from a charitable trust, which they now knew, of course, had been a front for VIGIL. Since its purchase, the building had spawned a number of modern appendages around its Victorian core: the Science block and the gym and also the theatre, of course, where Jack would be appearing in *Hamlet* in two weeks' time. It all seemed very normal. Just like all the other schools in the Borders, against which Angus regularly played rugby. There was one difference. Soonhope High housed the most advanced technology known to man: a working Taurus. A time machine. As a result, the site had tighter security than a US nuclear missile base. But it was completely unobtrusive. And that was the idea. Only a select few knew of the astonishing secret within the school walls.

The helicopter touched down and Jack, Angus, the Rector and Inchquin climbed out.

"Keep your heads down," warned the Rector.

In the distance, two familiar figures stood waiting to welcome them – their old friends, Tony Smith and Gordon MacFarlane. They waited at one of the school's side entrances. Tony took up almost the entire doorway. Gordon stood beside him. He was shorter but still built like a tank. Officially, they were the school janitors. But Jack and Angus had learned their true identity six months before. Along with Belstaff and Johnstone, they were part of VIGIL's elite security squad.

"Gentlemen, please escort these two through Entrance B to the Situation Room. We will join you shortly."

"An escort? Good." Angus replied. "You two should have blue flashing lights on your heads."

"That's funny, Mr Jud. Look," Gordon clutched his stomach with both hands, "I'm in stitches."

The Rector scowled. "Gentlemen, I would advise less levity. We have an extremely serious situation here. Do I make myself clear?"

Gordon looked at his toes, sheepishly. "Yes, Sir. Sorry, Sir."

Jack and Angus followed Tony and Gordon into the old Victorian part of the school.

"Right, here we are," Tony announced.

They had reached a store cupboard halfway along one of the main corridors and Tony proceeded to take a large set of keys from his belt, jangling them loudly as he searched for the right one.

"Isn't that a bit low tech for VIGIL?"

"Now, son," Tony replied in a hushed voice, "you know better than to mention that name in an open corridor, even if no one else is here. Anyway, it's all part of our image. You're not supposed to see all the high-tech stuff."

Tony located the key, inserted it into the lock and opened the door. The cupboard smelled of, well... school. That stale, dusty smell of textbooks, old bits of computer equipment and stationery. Tony reached inside his pocket and pulled out a thin piece of plastic, a bit like a pocket calculator. He gently pressed a button on the device and the cupboard door closed automatically.

"That looks more like it," Angus said, knowingly.

"I think this procedure will be familiar to you all. Step to the back, please," Tony said, pressing the device in his hand a second time. Without warning, an aperture formed in the floor. Soon the entrance had opened completely and a steep spiral staircase appeared, leading downwards. It was lit by a ghostly blue glow, just bright enough to make out the position of the steps.

"Okay – all clear – on you go."

One by one, they stepped onto the spiral staircase. The steps began to descend automatically. As they dropped beneath floor level, the aperture above them closed silently and after a couple of minutes they came to a gentle halt. Ahead of them was a door. Tony pressed the device again and it opened onto a short metal-clad corridor illuminated by the same dim blue light. At the end of the corridor was a circular door like the entrance to a bank vault. It had five letters etched on it: 'V I G I L'.

The door opened without a sound, revealing a tubular passageway that curved off symmetrically both to the left and to the right. Jack noticed that there were no markings on the passage walls – no rivets, no seams – it was perfectly smooth.

"Round to your left, please," Tony said. They followed obediently and as they walked, the passageway bent away from the entrance, which resealed itself silently behind them. They had only taken twenty or thirty paces when Jack noticed a strange marking on the wall at about head height. It appeared like the outline of a figure – a stylised hominid figure of some sort. There was something other-worldly about it. Jack stopped and turned to Tony.

"What does that symbol mean, Mr Smith?"

Tony approached the figure on the wall. He turned to Gordon. "Have you seen this, MacFarlane?" he said apprehensively.

Gordon moved closer and inspected the strange marking, running his fingers tentatively over it. "Mmmm – the latest experiments must be more advanced than we thought."

Tony turned back to Jack and Angus. "VIGIL have been using their wormhole technology to experiment on new applications..."

The boys' eyes widened.

"Yes – the figure on the door is indeed a symbol..."

"The alien symbol," Gordon added reverentially.

"Signifying a portal to a whole new universe."

Angus's eyes were on sticks, "You mean... space travel?"

Tony put them out of their misery, "No, you plonker, that's the Gents toilet – and the Ladies is opposite – look. Do either of you need to go?"

Gordon laughed raucously and the boys shuffled on their feet self-consciously.

"We're fine, thanks."

The party moved on, Tony and Gordon buoyed by their joke at the boys' expense.

Finally Tony announced, "Right, here we are."

The passageway had continued to curve round and they had reached a point where the grooving on the wall indicated another doorway. Jack reckoned that if they continued on they would eventually arrive back at the point where they had originally entered the underground complex. Essentially, they were in a giant subterranean doughnut from which all the various VIGIL control rooms and annexes could be accessed.

Jack read the lettering on the door:

'Situation Room'.

He felt his heartbeat tick up a notch. This was it.

Tony pressed the device in his hand and the door slid open.

On each wall of the large underground room there were screens – some showed maps, some complex-looking historical timelines and others just row upon row of computer programming language that Jack could not even begin to understand. Some of the VIGIL team were already seated around a large central board table. They looked like a war council. Others manned computer terminals, or scientific equipment, at pods in separate areas of the room.

Jack spotted a number of familiar faces: Miss Beattie, their English teacher, was involved in an animated conversation with, of all people, Gino Turinelli, from the café in the High Street. Jim De Raillar, who ran the mountain bike shop two doors down from Gino's, was also there and, finally, Jack's mother, Carole, was sitting at one of the computer terminals. In fact, as Jack looked around, he recognised everyone. They all either worked at the school or in the local village of Soonhope. Since their inauguration into VIGIL, Jack had learned that VIGIL's network was quite pervasive. It made sense. Clearly, you would need a lot of different skills to create and maintain a working time machine – especially if you ever happened to need to use it. Each member of VIGIL had their everyday persona: teacher, shopkeeper, janitor and so on. Then they had their other, secret, role in the VIGIL organisation – scientist, analyst, technician or security guard. For example, Jack had learned that Miss Beattie was not only an expert on Shakespeare, but also had a first class degree from Cambridge and had done stints at the Massachusetts Institute of Technology and the European Organisation for Nuclear Research – CERN. Gino – actually *Professor* Turinelli – was a computer expert, and Jim De Raillar and Jack's mother were analysts.

Just then, the Rector and Inchquin came into the room through a separate entrance. Soon a tense discussion was under way, facilitated by Inchquin who sat gravely at the head of the table.

"Jim, can you give us an update on the analysis of the message Tom Christie sent to us a couple of hours ago, please?"

"Certainly. To recap, the message confirms that Christie and Dr Pendelshape have fallen out. It also explains that following their failure to stop the First World War they started to work on a new timeline simulation some months ago..."

"What period does the simulation focus on?"

"Late Elizabethan."

"Interesting..." Theo Joplin, the historical analyst, interjected, and the Rector flashed him an angry glance for interrupting.

Day of Deliverance

Jim De Raillar ignored the comment and continued. "Anyway, it appears that the Revisionist team have refined the computer simulation software so they can make much more precise recreations of the interventions they plan to make in history, and the potential consequences of the action. Christie's message referred to it as 'surgical' historical modelling. It seems that the Revisionist team were very excited about these advances... but then Christie got nervous when Pendelshape started to talk in terms of progressing the simulation to the implementation phase – an actual intervention in history. Pendelshape wanted to target the late sixteenth century using their replica Taurus. Of course, it was clear from the message that Christie's greatest concern is for Jack's safety. He does not want the Revisionists to do this..." De Raillar looked at Inchquin and then at Carole and Jack uneasily. There was an edgy silence in the room.

"Carry on."

"Well, it appears that Pendelshape and the rest of the Revisionists do not share these concerns and it looks like they have decided to go it alone. Christie felt that the Revisionists had moved against him and he decided to leave them some weeks ago. Concerned that they would quickly refine the simulation and we might think him responsible, he took the unprecedented step of sending us a warning message today – and then contacting Jack directly by phone. It was a big step to take. Christie knows he is risking his life – betraying his own team in such a way. He is now isolated from both VIGIL and the Revisionists."

Inchquin arched his fingers in front of him, deep in thought. "So – Pendelshape has usurped Tom Christie as the leader of the Revisionists. He has a plan to make some intervention in history – in the sixteenth century. Okay, two things to check. First, Carole, what is the latest forecast on time signal availability?"

Carole looked up from her terminal. "We have had no time signal availability for a number of weeks now, but as you are aware, we are forecasting the availability of carrier strength time travel signals over the next forty-eight hours. Of course, forecasts are not accurate – in terms of timing, duration or strength."

"Time signal forecasting – it's worse than the weather forecast..." Joplin moaned.

"Shut up, Theo, you're not helping," the Rector said. "This is why Christie has chosen to contact us now. The Revisionists will also know that we are entering a period of potential time signal availability... so Christie must think they will use this opportunity to carry out their plan." He paused. "Do we have any details on the actual intervention in history that they are planning?"

"No. Apparently when Christie left them, there were a number of open scenarios still being analysed, but they were not complete. He had no final detailed plans."

"So, Theo, now is the time to say something sensible. You're the historian, any particular views on why they would choose the period between 1580 and 1600 to make an intervention?"

Theo Joplin looked up from a laptop that he had open in front of him. He was only twenty-seven but looked like a relic of sixties' hippiedom with his long hair, goatee beard and flowery shirt. But appearances were deceptive and encased within his mop of messy black hair was an encyclopaedic knowledge of history.

Joplin curled his lip. "A good choice if you want to make some structural changes to the future course of history – many, many options. Lots going on. Overall, a very cool period..." He turned back to his laptop assuming that this would be a more than sufficient contribution to the conversation.

The Rector tried to contain his frustration. "Would you mind being a little more *specific*?"

Joplin shrugged nonchalantly. "English Renaissance, Shakespeare, Marlowe, Spanish Armada – or Armadas – I should say, Mary, Queen of Scots, the Babington Plot, Drake, Raleigh, Howard, Grenville, Treasure Fleets, first English colony in America, religious conflict, Ireland... I could go on... and no doubt you'll want me to..."

"We don't have time for all this," Inchquin said irritably. "Jim, are we sure that Christie's message did not say anything more specific about what Pendelshape and the other Revisionists might be trying to do?"

"He said that Pendelshape had a well-developed theory that if the Spanish dominance of the period could be extended somehow, then it might be harnessed to usher in a period of peace. Perhaps for centuries. A strong Spain would have defeated the Netherlands and then colonised all of the Americas... and also they would have been better able to enforce a single religion – Catholicism. This would have reduced religious conflict."

"Interesting theory." Joplin was suddenly enthusiastic. "It's true that the period was a bit of a turning point for Spain. She was the most powerful country in the world, but her power declined – gradually mind you – pretty much from then onwards."

"Since when, specifically?"

"The defeat of the Armada, really, in 1588. The fact that Queen Elizabeth reigned for so long, as a Protestant queen, and the fact that the Armada failed meant that the balance of power – certainly naval power – slowly transferred to England, then to Britain. And by the nineteenth century, Britain was the most powerful nation on earth."

"So you're saying that if the Armada Campaign had succeeded, the world would have been a different place."

"Very different. The common language of the West would be Spanish, not English – just as it is in much of South America today. The influence of Protestantism would have been substantially weaker and we would have many different habits and customs. We might even have had a regular bullfight in Soonhope," Joplin chortled.

"Theo, this is not funny," Inchquin growled. "Jim, do you think Pendelshape's plan is to give power to the Spanish?"

"It's something along those lines – it marries up with Christie's communication to us. But the details clearly weren't fully developed when he left – so I don't think he knew the specifics. But the main thing he wanted to make clear was that he didn't want to be associated with any of it and, more than that, he wanted us to know that he was not associated with it so that we would not take retribution on him." Jim paused and then added bluntly, "Or his family."

"I understand," Inchquin said, moving on swiftly. "Well, we really need more data than this. It is all too sketchy at the moment. Tony, can you radio the team up on the hill? Perhaps they have managed to track him down…"

Suddenly, Carole called out from behind her terminal. "Councillor. There is some sort of reading. We have an emerging time signal. It's faint but it looks like there is a possible deep time disturbance… possibly time-travel initiation."

"Can you pinpoint it?"

"Difficult to identify it precisely – but the impacted year is 1587. Looks to be early on in that year."

"Location?"

"England – definitely. South-east. Must be London."

"Well that decides it then. It looks like Christie was right and the Revisionists are making their move. We must not waste any more time. We need to mobilise immediately." Inchquin rose to his feet and placed both palms on the table, his voice grave.

"I feared it would only be a matter of time before this happened again. Everyone – security protocol is Triple Alpha. VIGIL is now on high alert. You all know what to do."

Sixteenth-century Sortie

Jack stood in front of the Taurus. He felt different emotions. Not all of them good. Last time he had been in the Taurus control room, he had thought he was going to die. It loomed ominously behind a solid wall of thick green glass that extended from the floor all the way up to the ceiling. The great machine had been expanded and rebuilt since he last saw it. From their previous mission, VIGIL had learned that the Revisionists' Taurus was significantly larger than VIGIL's and had the capability to transport sizeable items of machinery, as well as people. In the last six months, work had been carried out on VIGIL's Taurus to ensure that it was up to scratch. However, VIGIL would only ever use their machine for emergencies such as this. They were reluctant to transfer equipment that was potentially out of period because of the historical consequences it could have. The Revisionists, they had learned, were not so fussy.

The great machine sat brooding among a complex assortment of engineering equipment – pipes, cables and access gantries. The shell of the Taurus itself was a raised metal platform bounded by a semi-closed arrangement of hefty, black metal struts. There were eight of them. They rose from the ground and bulged out to surround the platform and then they rejoined each other at the top. The simplicity of this structure belied the wonder and complexity of its function. This machine could take you back in time.

The VIGIL team quickly developed a plan based on piecing together the little information that they had gleaned from Christie's message to VIGIL. A party of four would be conveyed to February 1587 to attempt to locate and intercept Pendelshape before he carried out the Revisionist plan. This would not be easy, as the details of his intent and his location were sketchy. The search party on the hill had reported back and so far there had been no sign of Tom Christie. It was unlikely he would contact VIGIL again – there was too high a risk that he might reveal his own whereabouts. In any case, it seemed likely that he only knew the outline of the Revisionist plan. Nevertheless, Inchquin had instructed the search party to continue through the night.

The time-travel team had already been chosen: Tony, Gordon, Jim De Raillar and Theo Joplin had been dispatched to the preparation annex for equipment allocation and further briefing. It was not clear to Jack what would be done with Pendelshape in the event that he was found by the VIGIL squad, but he suspected that it would not be pleasant.

Inchquin had issued orders to power up the Taurus and the remaining VIGIL team members had already arrived to support the emergency mission. Everyone seemed to be well drilled – emergencies like this were something that they now practised for repeatedly, following the scare six months earlier. The control room itself had morphed into a fully kitted-out command centre. The nearest thing Jack could compare it to was NASA mission control. Jack and Angus sat in an observation area within the control room. Angus followed the proceedings with great excitement and would occasionally nudge Jack and point something out as the transfer time drew close.

As they watched, a door at the far end of the control centre opened and the VIGIL response squad arrived from the preparation annex, ready to board the Taurus.

"Best I could do, I'm afraid," Joplin announced.

The response squad needed to be fully prepared for the Elizabethan period. They had to ensure that they would not inadvertently trigger something, however small, that might have a knock-on effect in the future. If they did, VIGIL might need to return to repair the damage – a risky scenario in itself. They needed to try to blend in. At the basic level, this meant wearing the right clothes. VIGIL had built up an extensive costume archive for this purpose.

Day of Deliverance

The response squad stepped forward, somewhat sheepishly, to display the fruits of their efforts. Tony and De Raillar looked reasonable. They wore snug black doublets with jerkins on top and short cloaks. Beneath their cloaks, each carried a thin backpack that contained a range of equipment for their mission and some basic provisions. Their legs were clad in breeches that were pinned in at the knee. Each had a dagger on a belt. Joplin, however, looked like something out of *The Three Musketeers*. He wore a loose-fitting doublet with baggy trousers that were tucked in at boot level and a long, elaborately embroidered cloak that hung jauntily from one shoulder. On his head was a ridiculous wide-brimmed hat, adorned with a long plume of feathers, and on his feet were riding boots with wide, lace-trimmed turnovers. Finally, from a broad leather belt hung... *a full-length sword*.

"It's about forty years too late for the period – but it's all we could find in the wardrobe..." he announced.

But the best was still to come.

A moment later, when Gordon appeared, Jack and Angus burst out laughing. Gordon also wore a tight doublet on his upper body, but it was far too small for his powerful frame. The garment had elaborate inlays and patterns and, at the collar, Gordon's intricate lace ruff seemed to push his chin upwards at an alarming angle. On his legs, Gordon wore enormous baggy breeches that ballooned out from his waist and were gathered in at mid-thigh level. These were also highly decorated in a night-scape of yellow half-moons and stars. Angus and Jack had to rub their eyes because beneath the flouncy breeches, Gordon was actually wearing tights. *Bright yellow tights.* They encased a pair of powerful legs that were far better suited to pumping iron than mincing around an Elizabethan royal court. To finish it off, Gordon's white shoes were open on each side and – this was the final straw for Angus and Jack – *flowers* were pinned to the front. A *lot* of flowers.

Inchquin put his head in his hands. Gordon shrugged, "We ran out – had to move onto the aristocrat's section. At least I'm in period."

The Rector sighed. "You'll just have to see what you can lay your hands on when you get there."

With everything finally in place, the Rector completed the briefing. "Any questions before we initiate countdown sequence?"

Angus nudged Jack. He had a warped smile on his face, the kind that Jack knew typically meant only one thing – trouble.

Jack mouthed, "What?"

But before Jack could stop him, Angus was marching over to the Rector and Inchquin. "What about us?" he demanded.

Jack cringed. Without hesitation, Inchquin replied, "Out of the question."

But Angus was not about to be patronised. "So why are we in VIGIL at all then? You have always said that one of the main points of VIGIL is to prepare the next generation, you know, to protect history and protect the human race – how can we do that if we are stuck here – just watching?"

Suddenly, support piped up for Angus from an unexpected source – Miss Beattie. "You know the lad has a point. He's young, he's extremely fit and has already proved himself on one mission."

"Yes, Sir," Angus said, "I thought that was what I was here for, you know, to help."

Inchquin looked at the Rector and Miss Beattie nervously. "I'm not sure we can authorise... we are not really in a position..."

Angus interrupted him. "But you said yourself – VIGIL can decide whatever it wants."

Inchquin turned to his colleagues, waiting to see if any would voice an opinion. There was silence.

Angus's outburst had got Jack thinking – but not quite along the same lines as his friend. He spoke up. "Sir, I'm not as keen as Angus – I mean time travelling again would be pretty scary. But there is one thing. Angus and I know Pendelshape. And we also know that Pendelshape was desperate to get us to join him and Dad. I know Dad has had a bust-up with Pendelshape. But maybe if we were to go back as part of the team, maybe there would be a chance we could link up with Pendelshape and, well, pretend we wanted to come over to his side, you know, because of Dad or something. With us under his control, Pendelshape would think he could get Dad to rejoin the Revisionists. What I am trying to say is..."

Inchquin finished Jack's sentence. "Your old teacher might trust you... and we could use that to stop Pendelshape and infiltrate the Revisionists..."

"And finish them off for good," the Rector added. He nodded thoughtfully. "It certainly gives us another option."

Angus punched the air. "Yes!"

Inchquin smiled. "I guess you can take De Raillar and Joplin's places – they will form the next wave – your back-up, if it's needed."

Jack's mum had been following the discussion with increasing dismay. "I can't possibly agree to this..." she burst out.

But the words tumbled from Jack's mouth before he had time to stop them. "Mum – sorry – I've been thinking about it. The Christie family is partly responsible for all of this. If it's anyone's duty to help sort this out, it's got to be ours... mine."

It was decided.

Thirty minutes later, Jack, Angus, Tony and Gordon stood on the Taurus platform. Miss Beattie's costumes for the production of *Hamlet* were now period costumes for Jack and Angus. Beneath their woollen cloaks they each carried one of the thin VIGIL backpacks. Under their doublets, tight-fitting vests secured the all-important time phones. The countdown was already under way and the assembled VIGIL team looked on from their positions behind the blast screen. The Rector was completing a short lecture on the workings of the Taurus. Not that Jack needed reminding.

"Remember, the Taurus itself stays put – it focuses the energy and creates the temporary wormhole. But to move through time and space, you need to have physical contact with your time phone. You need it to go... and to get back again. While back in time, the time phones are controlled and tracked by the Taurus. Of course, they will only work when the Taurus is at the right energy state, and also when there is a strong enough time signal." The Rector had also reminded them of the limitations of the Taurus and its umbilical linkage to the time phones. "You can only use your time phone when you have a signal – and the signals are intermittent. Remember that bar?" He prodded the little greyed-out display inside the time phone. "When it's yellow – you're good to go – you can communicate, we know where you are and the Taurus can send you back and forth through time. When there's no signal, you're stuck, although the phone's energy source will continue to tell you where and when you are..." Finally, he said ominously, "Lose your time phones and there is no way back."

Jack was sweating. He could hear the high-pitched whine from the powerful generators, even though they were well insulated within the underground complex. He glanced across at Angus who stood next to him on the platform, grinning inanely, still not believing his luck. He didn't seem remotely concerned that he was about to be flushed down a wormhole to four hundred years in the past and a world that they would find totally alien. In front of them, Jack could see the small heads-up display. Taurus was counting down:

18... 17... 16...

Last time this had happened, Jack had been so frightened he had not noticed the physical changes around him in the Taurus chamber as they approached the event horizon – the point of no return. Around his feet he could see shimmering eddies of light. He supposed they were some sort of electrical disturbance, a bit like the ion-charged curtains of blue, red and green, that were known as the Northern Lights. The shimmering became stronger and it was as if he were standing in the rippling waters of an illuminated whirlpool. The atmosphere within the Taurus structure was also changing and the control room beyond appeared darker and fuzzier – as if you were looking at a badly tuned TV screen.

Suddenly, through the blast screen, he saw the Rector draw his hand dramatically across his throat, as if to say "Stop". He was shouting and waving frantically, and immediately there was a flurry of activity in the control room. The Rector's distorted words came through the audio feed.

Day of Deliverance

"Abort! Abort!"

There was something wrong. But the countdown just continued.

7... 6... 5...

Jack felt panic surge through his body and he glanced over at Tony and Gordon for guidance. But there was nothing they could do. They could hear the Rector's voice, desperately shouting, "Abort system – time fix malfunction... abort this mission – NOW!"

3... 2... 1

Jack looked down. Suddenly the flashing electrical whirlpool beneath them vanished and they were staring down into a black abyss.

The last thing he heard was his mum screaming, "Jack!"

Keep Your Head

Jack opened his eyes. He was lying on his back, staring into a bleak, grey sky. Suddenly, three large, golden lions floated gently across his field of vision. Jack blinked. It had happened. He was dead. He was in heaven; mystical golden lions were flying across the sky...

"Get up!"

Angus's ruddy face loomed over him as he shook Jack by the shoulders.

Jack blinked again. Then he understood. He was staring at a giant flag that fluttered in a strong, wintry breeze just above their heads. The flag was split into quadrants – the upper left and lower right quadrants had dark blue backgrounds, each displaying three identical symbols that looked a bit like flowers. The other two quadrants each had a crimson background on which appeared the three golden lions – the lions that Jack had seen as they fluttered in the sky above him. Jack recognised the design of the flag from Miss Beattie's book. They were English lions and French fleurs-de-lis. The English royal standard.

"I've no idea where we are, but there are loads of people down there..."

Jack pulled himself to his feet and rubbed his head. He felt like he'd been hit by a truck.

"What's going on? What..."

But Jack was silenced by the view in front of him. It took his breath away. They were perched on top of a vertiginous, crenellated tower which rose high above one side of a massive medieval castle. They could see for miles in every direction – a flat, sparse landscape of muddy fields, marshes and scattered woodland. There was no foliage on the trees and it was bitingly cold. The stonework beneath their feet was wet from a recent downpour. Below them – it must have been over a hundred feet below – a slow-moving river meandered gently through the countryside. Nearby, there was a fine stone church with flying buttresses and a distinctive octagonal tower. Jack could also see a large crowd of people stretching from the entrance to the castle, all the way back along a track towards a small village. Some people in the crowd were holding placards, as if they were at a demonstration. They were being chaperoned by men on horseback. It was difficult to make out what was on the placards, but there was one large one near the front that seemed to have a picture on it. It was bizarre, but Jack could have sworn it was a picture of a mermaid.

"Where are we? What happened?" Jack said, woozily.

"Don't know. I think we passed out. My head's thumping."

"Something went wrong."

"You can say that again. Tony and Gordon have disappeared, unless they landed somewhere nearby..."

"We're on our own?"

"Looks like it... some sort of malfunction."

"Are they dead?"

"No idea."

Jack's heart sank when the reality of their situation dawned on him. He gritted his teeth and swallowed.

"Well, we'd better get a grip. We're paid-up members of VIGIL now. Have you looked at your time phone?"

Angus slipped his hand beneath his cloak, inside the doublet and into the breast pocket of his under-vest. He unzipped a padded pouch and removed the precious time phone. Cupping it in his hands, he flicked it open. A faint blue light illuminated the device from the inside. They inspected the readout:

> **Date: Wednesday 8th February 1587**
> **Time: 9.45 a.m.**
> **Location: Fotheringhay, England**

Jack gasped. "Taurus has dumped us back in 1587 all right..."

Angus looked over the parapet, "But this doesn't much look like London. No red buses for a start."

"Right. Maybe that's why they tried to abort the mission? Maybe the Taurus put us here by mistake... maybe it even split us up and put Tony and Gordon in the right place?"

Angus groaned, "Well, what do we do now?"

"Is there a signal?"

"Be serious."

They peered into the time phone again. The telltale bar that burned bright yellow when there was a time signal was greyed out – dead. The boys knew what that meant. They were stuck. They couldn't communicate with home. There was no way of knowing how long it would be before they could get a signal.

"Well that's great. We're stuffed. Already," Angus said, bitterly. "So much for VIGIL."

"Here, let's have a look at that readout again."

Jack studied the readout and pondered its meaning. "Our location – Fotheringhay... and that date..."

Angus cocked his head. "Where is Fotheringhay, anyway?"

"It's not a hard 'G' by the way. It's a village in England. I think it's in Cambridgeshire or somewhere. I'm sure this place is famous... but I can't remember why."

"Well, we can't hang around here much longer. I'm freezing my butt off."

Angus was right. The adrenaline had finally worn off and it was a bitterly cold morning. It might even turn into snow later. They needed shelter.

"Down there, I suppose?" Angus nodded towards a small arched oak door built into the tower.

"Probably. I don't know what choice we have. Judging from that crowd, there seems to be some sort of big event going on in the castle. Maybe it's a marriage or something. We should be able to sneak out through the crowd."

"Then what?"

Jack shrugged. "I don't know. We probably need to try and hide somewhere until we get a time signal and can communicate with VIGIL. But you're right, we can't stay up here, we'll freeze to death."

The squat wooden door opened onto a dank spiral staircase and the boys started to make their way down. As they descended, a slit window occasionally gave them a view of the large courtyard at the centre of the castle. It was busy. Servants tended tethered horses while breast-plated soldiers and finely attired gentlemen talked conspiratorially in small groups. A large bonfire was being built and in one corner a cluster of musicians played a depressing dirge.

"Doesn't sound much like wedding music."

"No, and there seem to be guards or soldiers around, so something's going on."

"And that flag," Jack added. "I'm pretty sure it's the royal flag, so maybe it's a special occasion?"

"A royal visit? Now that would be something to tell Joplin – his goatee would drop off," Angus said.

They pressed on and finally reached the bottom of the tower, which opened through a large oak door onto a stone-flagged corridor. After following the corridor for a while, they heard hushed voices. A thick curtain hung in front of them. They looked at each other. There was only one way to go. Angus tweaked open the curtain and they slipped through.

They found themselves to the rear of a dense crowd in a large hall. People seemed to be jostling for position. Something in front was commanding a lot of interest, so nobody seemed to notice Jack and Angus. Soon, more people joined the crowd and they felt themselves being pushed further forward into the throng. There was woodsmoke in the air from log fires burning in the hall. It mingled with the smell of woollen cloaks – still wet from the early morning rain. Being tall, Angus had a chance of seeing what was going on, but Jack could see nothing – just the press of bodies in front of him. Pushing from behind propelled him forward and then, all of a sudden, he was at the front.

Below a great vaulted roof, a wooden platform had been constructed, fringed with black material. It looked about six or seven metres across and maybe half a metre high. It reminded Jack of the school production of *Hamlet* back at Soonhope, but it didn't seem likely that these people were there to watch a play.

Quite unexpectedly, from one side of the hall three men appeared, walking slowly. They were dressed in fine clothes and they looked important – they could possibly have been lords. The man in front carried a slender white stick. A tall woman walked slowly behind them with her head down. Wisps of her brown-auburn hair showed from underneath her headscarf. She was clad from head to foot in black velvet and a golden cross hung round her neck. As she appeared, the entire hall went silent.

The woman mounted the steps of the dais and walked to a high-backed chair, which was also draped in black. In front of the chair was a cushion and in front of that a simple wooden block with a half-moon shape cut into its upper section. The woman sat on the chair and for the first time raised her eyes towards the crowd. Two large powerfully built men stood either side of her. They reminded Jack of Tony and Gordon, but they were dressed entirely in black, and they wore masks. Angus peered at Jack with a quizzical look on his face; he had no idea what was going on. But Jack saw the implement one of the masked men held and he knew straight away. Both of the man's hands gripped the wooden handle of a large double-headed axe.

To their right, a clerk unrolled a parchment and started to read. The language was complicated but Jack caught snippets as the charge was read out, "Stubborn disobedience… incitement to insurrection… person of Her Sacred Majesty." The pieces of the jigsaw came together in Jack's head. The place: Fotheringhay Castle; the date: 8th February 1587; the crime: high treason; the punishment: death by beheading. Now Jack understood the significance of the placards outside the castle. The crowd outside were making their feelings clear about the prisoner before them in the Great Hall. Jack and Angus were about to witness the execution of Mary, Queen of Scots – cousin of Queen Elizabeth I and enemy of the English state.

The executioner and his assistant knelt before the queen to ask forgiveness. From where he stood, Jack could hear her reply word for word: "I forgive you with all my heart, for now, I hope, you shall make

The execution of Mary, Queen of Scots.

an end of all my troubles." Her ladies-in-waiting stepped forward to help her remove her gown. Beneath it she wore a satin petticoat – crimson – the martyr's colour. Next, she took the gold cross from her neck and handed it to the executioner, who slipped it into his shoe, claiming the executioner's right to the personal property of the condemned.

She knelt on the cushion and put her head on the block. Jack wanted to scream and turn and run. But the scene before them had a peculiar, hypnotic momentum and he was rooted to the spot, compelled to see the horror through to its conclusion. The white nape of the queen's neck stretched over the coarse wooden block for all to see. It looked strangely fragile and slender. She stretched out her hands to either side in the pose of Jesus crucified on the cross. The executioner wielded the massive wooden axe. It glinted momentarily in the firelight and then wheeled downwards with terrifying speed. The noise that the axe made on impact was one that Jack would never forget.

But the blow had failed to sever the head from the body completely and the executioner repeated the procedure. His job completed, he lifted the head from the floor and held it high crying, "God save the queen!" There was a ripple of noise through the crowd. The executioner was only holding Mary's auburn wig and the head, shaved to a grey stubble, had dropped to the platform and rolled forward before coming to rest not two metres from where Jack and Angus stood. Its pale eyes, still open, stared straight at them.

Escape

The bonfire in the courtyard was blazing and the crowd watched as Mary's garments were dispatched onto it. All clothes stained with her blood were to be burned to prevent them from being used as the holy relics of a martyr. Angus turned to Jack and spoke for the first time since witnessing the horror of the execution. His voice trembled.

"You're going to have to explain to me what we have just seen..."

"But not now; we need to work out how to get out of here."

"What about one of those?"

Angus nodded at the line of horses along one side of the courtyard. A number of them were saddled, ready for the gentry and noblemen. Many of those attending had been called at short notice to witness the execution, and some of them had ridden all through a rain-soaked night to arrive in time.

"I forgot you could ride."

"Of course I can ride – I live on a farm."

Jack wasn't sure this was something he wanted to hear. "But I can't."

"Easy – you just sit on the back. The horse does the rest."

"That's what I thought you might say. Anyway, those horses don't belong to us..."

Angus shrugged and turned back to the fire. Its warmth was little comfort.

"We need to do something. This crowd's starting to thin out – soon we'll be noticed. I've already had some funny looks."

They glanced around furtively. Across the other side of the courtyard, next to a large, arched doorway, they spied a group of men together with some servants. Jack jumped out of his skin when one of the servants seemed to point him and Angus out to an older, official-looking man. A moment later, three guards appeared from the doorway brandishing halberds. They advanced towards them.

"I don't like the look of this."

"Neither do I... we shouldn't hang around."

Without hesitation, Angus sprinted towards one of the tethered horses. He untied it, and, with impressive athleticism, jumped up onto its back.

There was a cry from the approaching soldiers.

"Spies! Stop them!"

Angus wheeled the horse round, "Come on – get up or we're done for."

"But..." Jack had no idea what to do; he'd never been on a horse in his life.

"Give me your hand."

Angus reached down with a swarthy arm and hauled Jack up towards him. Jack jumped and a moment later, to his great surprise, found himself sitting high up on the rear of the horse, behind Angus.

Angus wheeled the horse round and kicked in his heels. The poor beast reared up... for a moment Jack thought he was going to slide off – but then they rebalanced and the horse shot off at a gallop towards the castle gate. The remaining people in the courtyard leaped aside as Jack and Angus careered forward. Jack shut his eyes and clung on. There was more shouting from behind them. He braced himself. Was he about to get an arrow between his shoulder blades? Angus was going fast and they raced through the open gate and charged on along the lane that led up towards the village. Jack twisted round to see whether they were being followed. For a moment he saw nothing, but then a posse of four riders raced through the gate in hot pursuit.

"They're after us!" he yelled.

"Hang on!" Angus spurred the horse again and it pounded onwards. Jack felt he was going to be thrown off at any moment.

The village of Fotheringhay was small, but the dramatic events of the morning and its main street was swarming with people, animals and carts of all sorts. Angus slowed down a little and miraculously they managed to slalom their way through the throng. As they reached the far side of the village, Jack snatched a second look behind. The pursuing horsemen were still there – and they were getting closer.

He thumped Angus on the back. "They're gaining!"

The river came back into view on the left of the track. It was slow-moving but brown and swollen from the winter rain. Ahead, a wide bend in the river carved into the bank, forming a raised embankment of loose mud and gravel, high above the water. Angus veered towards it.

"Hold on!" he shouted. In a second, they were airborne as the horse soared from the earth embankment and plunged into the icy water. The cold took Jack's breath away. But the water only came up to their thighs and soon the horse found its footing on the bottom of the river. Angus made noises of encouragement – spurring the beast on. As they approached the opposite bank the current eased and the water became shallower. The horse sensed safety and pressed on energetically. They had made it.

Angus halted and wheeled them round. Opposite, their pursuers had arrived at the same spot on the high earth embankment. Immediately two of the pursuing horsemen attempted the same stunt. But the first horse slipped. Its rider became unseated and fell into the mud, sliding headlong into the torrent. The second horse somehow became entangled in the first and its rider was also thrown free. Soon both riders and horses were in the river, being swept along with the current. The two remaining horsemen waited at the top of the embankment. They were not about to risk the same fate and they peered across the water in frustration as Jack and Angus turned and galloped away to the woodland beyond.

The Fanshawe Players

The track became more gnarled and muddy the further on Jack and Angus travelled. It had been badly mauled by the wheels of carts and the hooves of horses, although they had seen nobody for at least two hours. A weak winter sun filtered through the oak branches above, but it brought no warmth and Jack's legs remained horribly cold from the dousing in the river. He was also aching from sitting awkwardly behind Angus on the horse which had kept going despite all the abuse thrown at it.

"We should let it go. It's not ours."

"What? And walk?"

"Maybe... though we may risk being caught – who knows what would happen then?"

"Probably a quick beheading."

"What do you think they wanted anyway?"

Jack shrugged. "I don't know. But they worked out we were strangers..."

"The guy said 'spy'. Why did he think that?"

"This is England, 1587, Angus. The queen has just ordered the execution of Mary, Queen of Scots, her own cousin. Mary was accused of a plot to overthrow Elizabeth; but I think there are plots going on all the time. Probably everyone is paranoid and jumpy... and with good reason. I read that the execution is the last excuse the King of Spain needs to launch the Armada – you know, to try and get rid of Elizabeth and Protestant England for good."

"Got to tell you – I'm not really bothered about all that. I want to get warm, get some food and wait for a time signal so we can make contact with VIGIL." Angus dismounted and patted the horse's grey flank. "Good boy."

"You can get off now, Jack. I think this lad's gone as far as he can." Angus patted the horse again. "What shall we do with him?"

"Let him go – he'll probably find his way back. Or someone will pick him up... he's valuable."

Angus slapped the rear of the horse and it trotted off back down the track. Jack looked around. The woodland was particularly thick here. There were a number of old oaks with impressively broad trunks. Even though it was winter and there was little foliage, they could not see through the woods more than about fifty metres in any one direction. It was eerily quiet.

"Hey, do your ears feel funny, Jack?"

"Sort of – but I think I know what it is."

Angus put a finger in one ear and rubbed vigorously.

"That won't help. It's nothing. I mean literally nothing. There's no noise. No ambient noise. Usually in towns and cities and even in the countryside where we live back home there is some sound or other – like from cars, planes, machinery and stuff. Usually you just don't notice it, but it's always there, in the background. Here, I guess there's none of that. It's perfectly silent. So it seems weird to us – almost sounds like there is noise."

"Well ambient whatsit or not, we need to push on for a couple of miles and then maybe turn off the road and go deeper into these woods. Find a spot to hide and wait – maybe try and get a fire going as we wait for a signal, or until the emergency rations run dry. I'm hungry, but we'll need to eke them out."

They continued up the track, trying to avoid the worst of the puddles and the mud, but progress was slow and soon their boots squelched with muddy water. After an hour, Jack was ready to give up when they rounded a bend which curved down to a small clearing in the woods. There was a muddy crossroads and to one side there stood a wooden cart, a bit like a gypsy caravan. It was the first sign of life they had seen since Fotheringhay. They approached cautiously. As they drew near to the back of the cart they could hear a sound. Snoring.

Suddenly, a man's face appeared from behind the canvas cover at the rear of the cart. It was a round face with red cheeks and it was cocked to one side. Rather oddly, the man was wearing a large, floppy jester's hat decorated with bright red and yellow stripes. It even had bells on it.

"Fanshawe! Monk! Get up!" he shouted in a squeaky voice. "We have visitors."

There was a commotion inside the cart and it creaked on its wheels. The donkey at the front chomped disinterestedly on the remains of the thin grass at its feet. Then, the faces of two other men popped out from behind the canvas cover. One was bald on top, with a fringe of straight black hair all the way round his head. The other was more distinguished-looking, and had a finely trimmed moustache and a pointed beard. He spoke in a rich voice and carefully enunciated each syllable.

"What have we here?"

Soon the strange trio of gentlemen were outside the cart and inspecting Jack and Angus with interest. The one with the jester's hat was actually wearing a full jester's outfit complete with diamond-patterned overcoat and pixie boots with bells on the toes. The bald one wore a simple brown cassock tied with a rope round his waist. The one with the beard – who seemed to be in charge – was dressed like a country gentleman with a doublet and hose, but he did sport a rather dashing green cloak.

"An audience perchance?" he queried.

Jack replied nervously, "Er, sorry, sir, we don't have any money..."

"We're on our way to..." But Angus didn't know where they could be on their way to and looked at Jack for inspiration.

Jack had a brainwave – he knew that Fotheringhay was quite near to Cambridge. "To Cambridge... we are... scholars. Returning scholars."

"Well there is a bit of luck – we are going to Cambridge as well," the man announced. He slapped his bald friend on the back, but the man just stood there, grumpily. "Monk – what do you think of that? These fine young men also journey to the city of Cambridge. Is that indeed not providential?"

At this exciting news the jester whipped out one yellow and one red handkerchief and proceeded to perform an astonishingly stupid jig for joy in front of them.

"We must be introduced. I am Harry Fanshawe." The country gentleman did an elaborate bow. "Leader of the Fanshawe Players..." he added grandiosely. "And this is Monk." Fanshawe elbowed the dour-looking man in the cassock. "Monk, try and be friendly." Monk grunted. "He's not a proper monk you know... it is just his *persona*... And this is Trinculo."

"At your service, sirs – will it be comedy, tragedy or poetry?" The jester grinned at them and made a low bow.

"Actually, we could do with something to eat," Angus said hopefully.

For some reason this made the dour Monk burst into sarcastic laughter.

"That's the best idea I have heard for two days." He suddenly stopped laughing, looked up at Fanshawe and asked, accusingly, "*Is there* any chance of some food... or even, dare I say it, some money?"

Fanshawe shrugged his shoulders huffily and spoke. "Fine then... I suppose I need to go and check the traps," he said, and marched off to the woods.

Despite the damp weather, Monk and Trinculo somehow managed to get a fire burning with kindling from the back of the wagon. Angus and Jack tried to help by gathering wood from the edge of the clearing. Although it was wet, the old stuff had been lying around for long enough that after the damp had smoked off, it caught light, and soon Jack and Angus were trying to dry their feet.

"He won't find anything," Monk moaned. "It's been two days now."

But then a triumphant Fanshawe appeared from a clearing, a brace of rabbits dangling from one hand.

"Providential!" he shouted.

Trinculo beamed. "Hallelujah!"

The rabbits were skinned at high speed – a spectacle that turned Jack's stomach, but seemed quite natural for Fanshawe, Monk and

Trinculo. Soon Monk was eagerly turning a makeshift spit suspended over the spluttering fire. Jack moved closer to the warmth. It felt good.

"So, gentlemen, you have not told us where you are from..." Fanshawe said, eyeing them curiously.

Angus looked over at Jack. "Er... the north."

"That must explain your strange accent. Which college in Cambridge will you be returning to?"

Again, Jack blagged an answer, remembering a name from Miss Beattie's book. "Queens' College..."

"A glorious establishment. Providential," Fanshawe said.

"And yourselves... where will you be performing?"

Fanshawe beamed with pride at the question. "We shall be performing with my friend the young genius, Christopher Marlowe."

Monk rolled his eyes cynically, "But he's not really your friend is he?"

Fanshawe's eyes flashed in anger. "A curse on you, Monk – he is my friend and he will welcome us with an open heart."

"Well let's hope he does – because if he doesn't, that's the last straw. I'm off, like all the others before me." Monk turned his attention back to the spit.

"Oh ye of little faith," Fanshawe retorted pompously. "Anyway, gentlemen, Marlowe," Fanshawe drilled his eyes into the back of Monk's head, "*my good friend*, will be performing his new play, *Tamburlaine the Great*, at Corpus Christi – his old college in Cambridge. And, what is more, he has invited the famous Fanshawe players to join him. It is the opportunity of a lifetime..."

"Opportunity of a lunchtime more like," Monk said sulkily under his breath.

Fanshawe ignored the remark, then added conspiratorially, "I hope that I might even sell him some of my work..."

"Your work?"

"Plays, sonnets and songs – a lifetime of toil and achievement. Even if I say so myself."

Monk rolled his eyes a second time, and Trinculo interjected before Monk said anything to further antagonise Fanshawe, "I think those must be cooked..."

The rabbit was removed from the spit and handed round. Jack and Angus exchanged glances, weighing up whether or not the meat would be safe, but the others were already munching away happily. Even Fanshawe had been momentarily silenced. Jack was so hungry he was past caring and he popped the meat into his mouth. It tasted rich, gamey and delicious.

In under a minute, the meat was gone but it had scarcely made an impact on their hunger. Angus proceeded to rummage inside his tunic and withdrew a small plastic bag. Jack shot him a look, but it was too late; the brightly coloured bag had already been spotted by the others.

"And what is this?" Trinculo asked. "An interesting bag of tricks?"

Angus looked down at the bag and suddenly realised his mistake. "Oh, sorry, a delicacy from our home, er, you know in the *north*. You eat them."

"Do they have a name?"

Angus glanced nervously at Jack, "They're called Jelly Babies."

"Babies of jelly?" Trinculo asked.

"Which you eat?" Monk said in awe.

"It's just a name – try one." Angus passed the bag round and, in trepidation, Trinculo, Fanshawe and finally Monk each removed one of the coloured sweets. Holding them in their dirty fingers, the three men waited for Angus to show them what to do. Angus shrugged and popped one into this mouth.

"There – nothing to it."

They each copied Angus, and, as they chewed expressions of wonder and appreciation spread across their faces.

"Sweet."

"Chewy."

"A most providential delicacy."

"Glad you like them. Here – have the rest."

The Jelly Babies were soon gone and Angus had made friends for life.

Fanshawe, probably buoyed by the unexpected sugar high, leaped to his feet to carry on where he had left off.

"My friends, I feel it is time for a song to celebrate our new friendship and a fine luncheon."

Fanshawe struck a pretentious pose and started to wail. Monk covered his ears.

"Sigh no more, ladies, sigh no more,
Men were deceivers ever;
One foot in sea, and one on shore,
To one thing constant never.
Then sigh not so,
But let them go,
And be you blithe and bonny,
Converting all your sounds of woe
Into 'Hey nonny, nonny.'"

Fanshawe's singing stopped abruptly and he looked around self-consciously. Jack realised what he was supposed to do and clapped heartily. "Well done!"

Angus joined in. "Er, very nice."

"A good effort, Harry," Trinculo said approvingly.

"Don't encourage him," Monk said. "It's taken him months to write that."

"You wrote it?" Jack said.

"But..." Jack was confused. He had heard the song before, in fact he was sure it was from Shakespeare. It was from another play they had done – they had even watched a film of it in class – *Much Ado About Nothing*. So how could Fanshawe have written it?

"You say you wrote it? This is part of your 'work'... and you say you have more?" Jack asked.

"You've done it now," Monk groaned.

But Fanshawe seemed to be delighted by the question.

"Of course, come, I must show you."

Fanshawe led Jack towards the wagon.

"This will interest you, my boy."

Jack jumped to his feet to follow Fanshawe. He briefly looked back at Angus, who shrugged his shoulders. Fanshawe climbed into the back of the wagon and Jack climbed in after him. It was stuffed full of clothes, bedding and other paraphernalia. It looked like it had been the Fanshawe Players' home, costume wardrobe and kitchen for months. It smelt bad.

"Over here."

They crawled towards the front of the wagon where Fanshawe unearthed a small wooden chest from under a pile of clothes.

"Here we are."

He took a large brass key that hung round his neck and inserted it into a lock in the front of the chest.

"Very precious."

Jack looked on, intrigued. Maybe Fanshawe was about to open a chest full of jewels or something – perhaps the lifetime takings of the Fanshawe Players.

Fanshawe opened the lid and Jack looked down on a pile of dusty old papers and parchment. Frankly he was disappointed.

Fanshawe beamed at Jack triumphantly. "There! What do you think?"

Jack did not quite know what to say. The reams of ink-stained paper were covered in a scrawly handwriting that was difficult to read.

"It's very nice... but I don't..."

Fanshawe interrupted. "Look, here is the first page."

Jack looked down at the piece of paper that Fanshawe held in his hands.

It read:

Mr Harry Fanshawe's Comedies, Histories and Tragedies.

Below this was a contents page entitled 'A Catalogue' and beneath this was a series of titles divided into three sections: Comedies, Histories and Tragedies.

Jack's brow creased in concentration. The titles on the contents page were familiar. Then his heart missed a beat when he realised what he was looking at. In amazement, he whispered to himself, "It's Shakespeare."

Fanshawe was still beaming, "I'm sorry my friend, it's what?"

Jack couldn't believe it. Fanshawe seemed to be in possession of an entire volume of Shakespeare's work. But... several years before Shakespeare had written them and over thirty years before they were compiled into a single printed edition of his work: the famous First Folio. Beattie had told them all about it. Back in the twenty-first century, there were only two hundred or so First Folios in existence. They were extremely valuable and sold for three million pounds or more. How could this possibly be in the hands of Fanshawe in the back of a mouldy old cart in the middle of a forest?

"Did you write all this?"

Fanshawe beamed proudly. "Every last word – that is my hand."

"But..."

Jack could not understand it. Was it possible that the failed actor – Harry Fanshawe, leader of a failed troupe of players – now on his last throw of the dice to somehow link up with the great Christopher Marlowe in Cambridge and save his career, could be the author of Shakespeare's works?

Jack scanned the titles on the page. He had the benefit of a quick mind, but he was certainly no expert on Shakespeare. He knew *Hamlet* of course, but only because they were putting it on at school in a couple of weeks. He didn't really know too much about the other plays, except what Miss Beattie had drilled into them in class. Nevertheless, as he scanned the titles in the contents page he realised that there was something wrong.

He recognised the titles as Shakespeare's... but not quite. It was as if they were not right, somehow. There were titles like:

Love's Labour's Not Quite Found;
The Twenty-two Gentlemen of Verona;
The Big Storm;
Much Ado About an Absence of Something;
All's Well that Ends Much Improved;
A Midsummer Night Amongst the Fairies;
The Tragical Historie of Dave, Prince of Denmark.

Day of Deliverance

It was apparent from the titles, that even if Fanshawe had spent a lifetime creating the work now ascribed to Shakespeare, he had perhaps not done it very well. It needed work – a lot of work.

"Incredible," Jack murmured.

"You're too kind." Fanshawe basked in what he took to be Jack's admiration. There was precious little of that coming from either Trinculo or Monk – whose patience with the whole Fanshawe enterprise was wearing thin.

"Do you think I could have a look at one of the plays?"

"Certainly, sir. Which one would you like to see?"

"What about that one – *The Tragical Historie of Dave, Prince of Denmark*."

"Certainly, my latest and proudest achievement." Fanshawe rummaged through the papers and drew out a sheath of ink-blotted papers. "Here we are."

Jack thumbed through the pages to find what he was looking for – Act III, Scene I – early on. Jack scanned the page. He knew the words he was looking for off by heart, so even in Fanshawe's unfortunate scrawl he should be able to spot them.

He muttered to himself, reading down the list of names, "Polonious, then the king, then Polonious... this should be it... and then... Dave?"

Jack looked up at Fanshawe. "Dave?"

"Yes – David – one of the main characters in this tragedy."

"Hold on, you've called him David...?"

"That is his name."

"Not Hamlet."

Fanshawe nodded thoughtfully. "Well, Jack, certainly 'Hamlet' has a certain ring to it... Yes – you're right... Hamlet... I like it! In fact now you mention it 'Dave' does not sound right at all! Let's make it Hamlet. Much more, er, *Danish*. Providential!"

Jack began reading the great soliloquy – one of the most famous passages in the English language. But they weren't the words he remembered or expected:

To be, or not to be; ay, there's the point
To die, to sleep, is that it? Yes – that's it;
No, to sleep, to dream. Ay marry, and off we go…

Jack could hardly bear to read on. It was complete rubbish. "It's gobbledegook."

"Yes – I agree," Fanshawe said. "I don't know what that word means, Jack, but I certainly agree with you – it is certainly one of my favourite passages… certainly gobbledegook."

Jack murmured, "It's Shakespeare, but not quite as we know it."

"Harry – can I suggest a couple of changes… for example, why not try the following?"

Jack closed his eyes and recited the words that he knew so well:

"To be, or not to be: that is the question:
Whether 'tis nobler in the mind…"

Jack completed the famous speech that he had rehearsed so much for the school play. Fanshawe looked at Jack with an expression of complete and utter awe.

"You have a gift… a gift of genius… a gift from heaven itself. How…?"

Jack smiled, "Oh I guess I'm a bit like you, Fanshawe, you know, a knack with words."

Fanshawe's eyes were agape. "But this is truly incredible… you have talent my boy… providential talent."

Jack blushed. He knew he probably should not have done it. "Really, it's nothing."

But before Jack could say anything, Angus stuck his head through the curtains at the rear of the wagon.

"You guys going to be long? 'Cos we got a problem. A big problem."

Bandit Country

There was something feral about the three men who stood on the track in front of them. Their faces and clothes – rags more like – were filthy. It was as if they had emerged from the undergrowth of the surrounding forest and were in some way part of it. Two of them brandished large wooden clubs, and the third a long knife. It was this third man who spoke through a toothless mouth.

"We don't want much..." he said. "Just everything you've got."

Trinculo was shaking and the bells on his hat started to tinkle.

"We have nothing," Fanshawe announced bravely, puffing out his chest.

But no sooner had the words come from Fanshawe's mouth than the ringleader wielded his great wooden club. It cut through the air and caught Fanshawe hard on the side of his thigh. Fanshawe wailed and collapsed to his knees, whimpering.

"We haven't time for this... Stave, search the cart... Butcher and me will see what this lot have on them." He immediately reached down to Fanshawe's neck and yanked off a thin silver chain and cross that hung there. "That'll do nicely for a start."

Fanshawe sobbed louder.

Suddenly, Fanshawe's small wooden chest was thrown from the back of the cart and Stave jumped out after it.

"I found this."

He booted the chest which flew open and Fanshawe's precious papers scattered across the muddy ground.

Fanshawe wailed hysterically.

The ringleader prodded him with his stick. "Shut your mouth – or you'll get more of this."

He strode over to the chest. "What is it?"

Trinculo and Monk were silent.

He turned back to them and snarled, "I asked what is it?"

Monk said quietly, "Plays, poems."

Trinculo mumbled, "They're not worth anything."

But the ringleader had a glint in his eye. "Not what I hear. You can get *ten shillings* for a play... maybe more, if it's any good."

The bandits gathered round the papers, suddenly interested.

Jack whispered to Angus from the side of his mouth, "Any ideas?"

"Tony and Gordon carried the only weapons, but I did manage to sneak this with me... was at the bottom of my school bag for some reason."

Angus opened his doublet fractionally for Jack to see what was inside. He had brought his catapult. And it wasn't the one made from a bit of wood hewn from a tree with an elastic band attached. Angus had a slingshot of high-tensile industrial rubber tethered to a carbon fibre frame. Jack had seen Angus use this favourite 'toy' to shatter a beer bottle fifty metres away. He opened up the other side of his doublet.

"And I found a couple of these in the VIGIL prep area... pocketed them while the others weren't looking," he whispered.

A couple of tubes poked up from his inside pocket. Jack didn't know what they were.

"Thunder flashes," Angus said guiltily.

The bandits had become bored with the papers and they hurriedly stuffed them back into the wooden chest. The ringleader turned back to them.

"What else have you got?"

Angus reached into his pocket, pulled out one of the thin tubes and held it out.

"I have this... But I don't know if you will want it."

"What is it?"

Angus looked at Jack who interjected, "We use it in our plays... it is, er, a musical stick. It makes music."

"Loud music," Angus added.

The ringleader came closer. "I have never heard of such a thing... how does it work?"

Day of Deliverance

"Easy," Angus said. "See that rock over there. Well, you just bang the bottom of the music stick on it... and then hold it in your hand... and wait for the music."

Stave barged forward. "I want to do it!"

"No me..." Butcher said.

"Stand aside – I will do it – I am the leader."

The ringleader took the thunder flash, marched over to the rock and manfully banged one end onto the rock. "Like that?" he asked.

"Yes," replied Angus, "just like that."

They waited.

The ringleader looked at them questioningly. "It's not work—"

Suddenly, there was a blinding flash of light and an ear-splitting bang as the thunder flash went off in the bandit's hand. It was as if the entire forest had gone up. For a second he was invisible in the swirling blue smoke, but as it cleared, the man staggered blindly around, clutching his hand and wailing in pain.

His friends raced over to help him. Angus whipped out his catapult and selected a stone from the ground. In one movement he stretched back the rubber, extending it all the way from his outstretched arm to his ear lobe. He closed his left eye and narrowed his right along the length of the rubber and... released. Jack could have sworn he heard the stone hiss angrily through the air. It caught Stave in his kneecap and he sank to the ground, emitting a low guttural grunt. Butcher turned, his face red with anger, and pelted towards them wielding his club as he came. But Angus had coolly reloaded the catapult and unleashed a second shot. It was extraordinary that a small pebble could stop a grown man in his tracks. But it did. Angus had again skilfully targeted the leg, and now all three of their assailants were on the ground. Alive, but in a great deal of pain.

Angus reloaded for a third time, but Jack put his hand up.

"I think we're done."

Angus lowered the catapult.

Fanshawe was soon on his feet, wrapping Angus and Jack in a bear hug.

"Thank you, my friends."

Trinculo immediately performed another jig – just as embarrassing as the first.

Jack and Angus approached the three bandits who groaned in the mud.

"Will they be okay?" Jack asked.

"Unfortunately, yes, they'll be limping around for a day or two... and what's-his-face will have a nasty burn on that hand... but they'll be fine."

Jack looked down at the three men. He wasn't quite sure what to say, but tried his best tough-man voice. "Right you lot. Come near us again... and well... we've got a load more tricks up our sleeves... and you'll regret it – we'll, er, be calling 999."

Angus tried not to smile. The bandits looked up at them with a mixture of confusion and fear. They seemed to have got the message.

They made the long approach to Cambridge from the north-west in the afternoon of the following day. Despite being trouble free, the journey had been tough and progress painfully slow along the pitted roads. They had taken it in turns to ride up on the cart... but most of the time they had walked. Since their impromptu lunch they had eaten very little, although Jack and Angus had, on occasion, dipped surreptitiously into their emergency rations. It was only because of this that they had managed to keep going and Jack had no idea how the others had survived the journey.

Despite little food, Fanshawe had babbled incessantly. Subjects included their miraculous escape from the bandits, the details of which Fanshawe and Trinculo repeated again and again, their exploits becoming braver and more exaggerated each time. Angus, in particular, was being likened to a demigod for his role in beating off the attackers. Even Monk added grudging words of thanks. Then Fanshawe turned to his great plans for the future of the Fanshawe Players and how, working with the young genius whom he had 'discovered' – one Jack Christie – they would all become famous and make their fortunes. Finally, he talked enthusiastically about their forthcoming meeting with Christopher Marlowe and their final destination, the town of Cambridge. As he called it, "The most exquisite in all of Christendom."

As they finally crossed Magdalene Bridge into Cambridge, Jack got a sense of why Fanshawe had been so animated at the prospect of visiting the town. To his left, the red brick buildings of Magdalene College stretched gracefully out along the River Cam. To his right, he set eyes upon a number of beautiful stone buildings and the spires of churches, which rose gracefully above the rooftops. The town was a stark contrast to the dirty hovels and huts that they had passed on their journey from Fotheringhay. They pressed on into the centre and the crowds became thicker. The streets were busy and they frequently had to navigate their way past oncoming carts or gaggles of students, hawkers or even monks. They turned right and passed St John's College and then Trinity College with its Great Court. As they progressed it was as if each building became bigger and grander. Finally, they reached King's College Chapel, a magnificent stone building, which towered fifty metres into a grey sky, eclipsing everything else around it. At each corner stood a high tower and there was a glorious stained-glass window built into the front elevation – itself nearly twenty metres high. Soon they were all gazing up in wonder at the great building, even the irascible Monk.

After a little while, they walked on, past the entrance to King's College until, finally, Fanshawe announced, "We're here."

To his left Jack peered through an archway into the courtyard of yet another college. It was certainly not as large or as grand as the great colleges they had passed already, but it was still very beautiful. Opposite the arched gateway, Jack could see an elegant chapel set into the college buildings.

"Is this Corpus Christi College?"

"Yes – this is where we will meet my friends and I have made arrangements for us to stay. You can make your way down to your lodgings at Queens' later. First things first, however – we must see to the cart and donkey..."

As they got themselves organised, they were distracted by a group of young men who approached from further down the street. They appeared to be in good humour and were singing loudly. They had been drinking. As they neared the college gate, Fanshawe went up to one of the men, who had wavy auburn hair and wore a black cloak with large buttons. He was a young man with a roundish, pale face, a light moustache and beard – not unlike Fanshawe's. He was unstable on his feet and he put out one hand to steady himself on the college wall.

"May I help you, sir?" Fanshawe asked the man. Fanshawe looked a little closer, peering into the man's face, his brow furrowed. "Marlowe? Christopher Marlowe?"

Marlowe looked back at Fanshawe, blinking and trying to focus his eyes. He let out a strange, strangled giggle, swayed again and was violently sick.

Corpus Conundrum

They were standing in the great wood-panelled hall of Corpus Christi College. Dinner had finished and Marlowe's group of players had been permitted to clear the far end of the hall to complete an evening rehearsal of his new play, *Tamburlaine the Great*. The arrival of Jack, Angus, Fanshawe, Trinculo and Monk had caused quite a stir among the players. Contrary to Monk's expectation, Fanshawe was well known to Marlowe and a number of his actors. They had been welcomed (particularly as there was a shortage of extra soldiers for the play); however, things were not going according to plan.

Marlowe himself, having been sick at the college gates when they met, was now flat out on the floor at the far end of the hall, sleeping off a heavy afternoon in the nearby pub, The Eagle. Meanwhile, the actor playing Mycetes, enemy of Tamburlaine, was rapidly following Marlowe into a comparable stupor, having discovered the key to the wine cellar beneath the hall. In addition, progress had been further delayed, as Marlowe had insisted that, in order to mark the occasion of the first public performance of *Tamburlaine*, he would arrange for a local artist to paint a portrait of the group. Prior to each rehearsal at college, the painter had lined up the entire cast in full costume and started scratching away at his easel. He was fussy and temperamental and the arrival of Fanshawe, who insisted that they should also be in the picture, had nearly caused him to walk out. Reluctantly, he had been persuaded to stay and the group posed appropriately, with Jack and Angus off to one side.

Once the actors had been standing for forty minutes they were starting to get bored and impatient to get on with the rehearsal. It had also become apparent that Mycetes had, in fact, smuggled an entire case of wine from the cellar and was happily circulating bottles around the group. Gradually the noise level increased and the behaviour and language became increasingly coarse. When half a loaf of bread left over from dinner flew from one side of the hall to the other, rapidly followed, in the opposite direction, by a large lamb chop, Jack felt it was probably time to leave. He didn't want to be there when the college master turned up to witness them in the middle of that most ancient of university traditions – the drunken food fight.

Jack nudged Angus. "Think it's time to move."

"Just when it was getting interesting."

Jack turned to Fanshawe, who seemed to be the only one taking a rather dim view of the proceedings. "Harry – shouldn't we see how Marlowe is doing... remember your plays... you wanted to show them to him?"

Fanshawe, and the faithful Trinculo, needed no excuse and they slipped over to the far end of the hall where Marlowe lay, still snoring loudly. They woke him and he slowly regained his senses. He pulled himself to his feet and stood unsteadily, clutching his head and groaning.

"What happened?" he asked woozily, gazing across at the melee in the hall. Monk had compensated for weeks of starvation rations by satiating himself with food and wine. Then, somehow, he had managed to suspend himself from the chandelier that hung from the centre of the vaulted ceiling. He now swung gently to and fro, slurping from a bottle.

The artist finally packed up his things and marched towards them in a furious temper, the unfinished canvas under one arm.

"I will send you the bill," he announced as he flounced past. Jack caught a glimpse of the unfinished painting as it swished before them, and saw a preliminary outline of Fanshawe, Trinculo, Monk, Angus and himself.

Marlowe groaned. "No chance of rehearsals now. In fact, there will be beatings at the buttery hatch for this mess, for sure." A sudden look of concern washed over his face. "But come, we have more pressing business. We should retire to my rooms."

Day of Deliverance

Marlowe had acquired two adjoining rooms in the college and the embers of a log fire still smouldered in the grate. Despite this, the room remained icily cold. Fanshawe stoked up the fire and added a couple of logs, which sparked to life. The room was a mess – papers and clothes were strewn everywhere. As Marlowe sobered up, it became increasingly apparent that he was nervous about something. When they had met that afternoon, he had been blind drunk and seemed not to have a care in the world. But now he was different. On entering his rooms he had carefully locked the door behind them and peered furtively from the window down to the quad below. Next, he had reached for a large bottle of brandy, which sat in front of them on a small wooden table. Having only just recovered from one drinking bout, he nevertheless poured some brandy into a glass tumbler and drank the whole lot in one go before refilling his glass. He then reached for four more tumblers and filled them all to the brim. Jack remembered Beattie's translation of the words beneath Marlowe's portrait in her book: *What feeds me destroys me.*

In fact, the playwright looked a bit like his portrait. He had intelligent eyes, wavy brown hair, a round, somewhat pallid face and a thin moustache and beard. Jack felt he should be in awe of the man who had so influenced the theatre. But instead Jack found himself surprised by his youth. Marlowe was only twenty-three – scarcely eight years older than Jack. It was hard to think of him as a great literary figure. Jack remembered that in only four years Marlowe would be dead – killed by a dagger stabbed just above his right eye in a brawl. As Miss Beattie had said, many thought it was murder – or even an assassination – brought about by Marlowe's love of risk-taking, or perhaps the rumour that he was a spy or double agent caught up in the dark world of Elizabethan espionage. Jack wondered whether he should inform the great man exactly how and when he would die and whether, in fact, this would accelerate or slow his creative output.

Promptly, Marlowe emptied his glass for a second time, leaned back into his chair and stared at the ceiling with an expression of deep concern, then his face suddenly changed and he let out a strange, manic giggle. Clearly, the great Christopher Marlowe was slightly unhinged.

"... and this is another of my favourites – a play about Scotland – it's called *MacGregor*." Fanshawe tried to puncture Marlowe's pensive mood by presenting some of his own work. He had brought his chest of papers up to the room to show Marlowe, hoping that he might generate sufficient enthusiasm to close a sale. Marlowe leafed through the papers, but he was too distracted.

"I am sure it is good work, Harry, but as you know, more work is the last thing I need, at the moment..." Again he giggled, and the noise sounded strangely out of place.

Fanshawe looked crestfallen.

But Marlowe remained untouched. "I am so busy with my own material... and we are just starting *Tamburlaine*..." He thought for a moment. "Although, I do hear that there is a young writer in London, eagerly looking for new material, I may even proffer some of my own... He is ambitious and quite well connected, I understand."

Fanshawe's eyes lit up. "London? What is the young man's name?"

"I am not sure I remember." Marlowe closed his eyes for a moment. "Shake-Shaft, I think, yes that was it, Wilbur Shake-Shaft..."

"I understand he frequents the Cross Keys Inn in Grace Church Street... I have had some correspondence with him."

Suddenly Marlowe stopped talking and leaped to his feet. Jack had heard nothing, but Marlowe, in his heightened state of paranoia, seemed to be attuned to the smallest noise. He rushed over to the window and again peered out from behind the curtain.

He wheeled round. His face was pale.

"They're here. They must have seen you. I feared this might happen."

He rushed over to a small desk on the opposite side of the room and frantically fiddled a key into the lock on a draw. He opened it and rummaged inside. He pulled out a folded document sealed with red wax on one side. His hand shook as he held out the document.

"Fanshawe – we have been friends for a long time. You must help me, I beg you."

Jack and Angus looked at each other anxiously.

"What is..." Fanshawe started to speak, but Marlowe interjected, his words hurried.

"Guard this document with your life... you must take it to Walsingham – only he can see it. Do not open it – it is sealed, so he will know if it has been tampered with."

Fanshawe's eyes were on sticks, "You want me to deliver this to Sir Francis Walsingham? But..."

"Yes, yes... Sir Francis Walsingham, the queen's secretary – at court," Marlowe confirmed in frustration. "It is of national importance. If they find it here with me they will suspect me and surely kill me..."

"But?"

"Do not question me... no one will know that you have it. Go now and you will be safe, and if the document is put securely into Walsingham's hand, he will reward you handsomely." Marlowe reached into a pocket and took out a small velvet bag. "Here's gold for your trouble, take it."

They heard the sound of heavy boots tramping up the stairs and, despite the temperature of the room, Jack saw small beads of sweat materialising on Marlowe's forehead. He looked around, desperately.

"I know!"

He led them into the small adjoining bedroom and opened a window. The cold winter air rushed in.

"Go out here, the college roof is just up there. You can make your way down on the other side. Don't worry, it's easy and it will be quiet. You have more than enough now to get you to London safely... and then to Walsingham."

"But what about my work?" Fanshawe said, looking at the chest of papers which still lay beside the table.

Angus rolled his eyes and started to snatch the papers from Fanshawe's chest. "Here – stuff them in our backpacks. We'll take what we can... come on..."

Jack started to help Angus while Fanshawe moaned about the pages getting torn or damaged.

"Stop fussing, we don't have time," Angus hissed.

Suddenly, there was a thunderous bang on the door and a heavily accented voice called out, "Marlowe – who is there?

Marlowe was already bundling Fanshawe and Trinculo through

the window. There was a loud bang as a firearm discharged right outside the door.

"That was a gun – I'm not hanging around any longer." Angus jumped up and out through the window, hot on the heels of Fanshawe and Trinculo.

Marlowe passed back into the main room as Jack climbed up onto the windowsill, following the others. Ahead, Jack could just see Angus's frame silhouetted against the light of the moon as he scrambled out from Marlowe's window and onto the roof of the college. Jack glanced back over his shoulder into the main room and saw the door fly open. For the last time, Jack heard Marlowe's nervous giggle. He turned and fled through the window and into the night, without waiting to see Marlowe's fate.

Night Climb

They raced across the roof of Corpus Christi College. A full moon washed the chimneys and crenellations in a shadowy monochrome. Jack's eyes adjusted quickly. He could soon see well enough to be sure of his footing and follow the others ahead of him.

"This way!"

Angus waved them forward and Jack saw him clamber up and over a wall that abutted the far end of the college roof. A secured ladder led to another roof below and Fanshawe and Trinculo followed Angus down it obediently. Jack paused to catch his breath. Behind, he could still see the yellow glow of candlelight from Marlowe's rooms. Suddenly, he saw an unfamiliar figure clamber out from the window and up onto the roof – just as they had all done, minutes before. He was quickly followed by a second figure – more squat, but powerfully built. They were being followed – presumably by the people who had shot through Marlowe's door. Jack couldn't work it out. They had not seen Jack and the others escape onto the roof, so Marlowe must have shown the intruders where they had gone. Why on earth would he do that?

Jack crouched down low. Although the roof was long and the men were still some fifty metres away, there was little cover and the light of the moon picked out Jack's outline against the low-rise wall that edged the roof. The first man was now straddling the apex of the roof. He stopped and appeared to reach for something strapped to his back. In the poor light, Jack could not see what it was, but the man brought the object forward and up to eye level, then pointed it directly at Jack. There was a loud *thwack* and almost instantaneously a small chunk of masonry dislodged from the wall behind Jack. A metal object rebounded from the brickwork and then clattered back onto the roof slates and rolled down towards the guttering. It was a crossbow bolt –

Jack realised he was being used for a bit of early evening target practice.

He immediately clambered over the wall and down the ladder to the lower roof, following the others. He could see that they had already made it down to the street and from below Angus waved him towards a heavy drainpipe. Jack scraped and slipped down the wall, using the drainpipe for support until he finally reached the street. He felt as if his head was going to burst.

"Can't stay here," he panted, waving up towards the roofline. "We've got trouble. Those men from Marlowe's rooms are following us. I've no idea what's going on but he must have put them onto us – no idea why. They've got crossbows; one of them took a shot at me."

"Who are they... what do they want?" Fanshawe whimpered.

"They're trouble, Harry, just like your 'friend' Marlowe. He's got us deep into something and I don't want to stay to find out what," Trinculo said.

"Let's go towards the town centre... probably safest if we can find a crowd," Jack said.

Just then, the air above them hissed and a second crossbow bolt embedded itself in the side of a wooden cart that was parked against the college wall.

"Hang around and we are going to get killed."

Turning from the side street, they raced back past the entrance to Corpus Christi and towards the great towers of King's College Chapel, which loomed into view on their left. There seemed to be quite a gathering of people at the college gate and they could hear the choir singing in the chapel beyond.

Jack spotted their chance. "Mix in with these people going to the chapel... must be a service or something..."

Joining the crowd, they slowed to a brisk walk, so as not to stand out. Soon they were through the gatehouse and walking across the quad towards the entrance of the vast, gothic chapel. Their path was illuminated by burning lanterns either side of them. Jack looked back. It was difficult to see clearly as there was a queue of people... but then, coming out of the gatehouse, about thirty paces behind them, he was sure he recognised the shapes of their two pursuers. Jack felt a burning urge to break and sprint away from the crowd, which slowed as it approached the chapel. He knew if he did, the men would be onto them immediately. The chapel was now right in front of them, soaring into the night sky like some vast container ship. There was safety in the queue of people as they inched their way forward, agonisingly slowly.

At last, they were inside. The great chapel was only lit by the gentle flicker of candles, but even by this light Jack could see that the building was magnificent – a huge rectangular cavern with clifflike walls and windows soaring up to a spectacular fan-vaulted ceiling way, way above.

Angus elbowed him in the ribs. "Wake up – what now?"

People were milling about and gradually taking seats for the service. They had minutes at most before their pursuers followed them inside the chapel.

"What about over there?" Angus whispered. He pointed to a small wooden door set into the wall in a corner of the chapel.

"Worth a go. But don't get noticed."

They moved quietly over to the door, aided by the shadows inside the chapel. While the others formed a screen, Jack tried the handle.

"It's open!"

Jack eased the door ajar and, checking that no one was watching, they each slipped into what seemed to be a large, dark cupboard. Except it couldn't be a cupboard, because grey moonlight glimmered through a narrow slit window above them.

"What is this place?"Angus whispered.

"It's the bottom of one of the chapel turrets – look, there are stairs," Fanshawe replied.

"Do you think anyone saw us?"

"I don't know, it was pretty dark in there, but we don't want to risk it. Let's go."

Jack started to climb the narrow spiral staircase. After a few minutes they reached a second wooden door that opened onto the massive roof of the chapel. The turret was one of two at the west end of the chapel that looked out over the River Cam. On the opposite side of the roof soared the taller twin turrets built into each corner of the east end of the chapel. They stood in silence in the doorway at the top of the spiral staircase, straining to hear any sound from below.

"Hear anything?"

The choir had stopped singing and the congregation below were still, awaiting the start of the service. Suddenly, they heard a scrape of ghostly footsteps echoing up the staircase towards them.

"They're coming – we've had it," Angus whispered, panic in his voice. "We can't go back down there and there's no way off this roof."

Jack smacked his forehead in a moment of inspiration. "The other turrets. They must have staircases too! We could go back down one of those."

Angus smiled. "Nice one."

The four of them dashed across the roof towards the turrets on the east side. Angus rattled the door handle of the north-east tower.

"It's locked!"

"So try that one." Jack pointed at the south-east turret and they clambered up over the crest of the roof and down towards it. It was a cold night, but Jack's palms were sticky with sweat. He turned the handle of the door in the south-east turret.

"Locked too. We're stuffed."

"Those guys will be up on the roof in no time. We're trapped…" Angus said between his teeth.

"And I don't want a crossbow bolt in my head," Fanshawe said, trembling.

"Unless…" Angus craned up at the massive octagonal turret that towered above them, tapering into the darkness of the night sky.

"No way…" Jack said.

"We don't have a choice – I don't want to be around when those guys get here. It looks easy enough – all those vent holes and gargoyles or whatever they are. We don't need to go all the way up, just to that parapet thing in the shadows so they can't see us…"

Jack took a deep breath and turned to Trinculo and Fanshawe. "We have no choice. The crest of the roof will give us some cover for a few minutes as we climb."

"But…"

Jack was frightened, but he felt himself getting angry. "Get a grip, Harry, or we're all dead. Do exactly what Angus does… and don't look down."

Angus stepped off the roof balustrade and onto a sloping slab of stone a few feet up the turret.

"It's not bad, the stone is easy to grip," he whispered down.

Fanshawe, Trinculo and then Jack started to follow Angus up the outside of the turret, placing hands, feet and even their whole bodies in exactly the positions that Angus showed them. They were pumped up with adrenaline and progress was surprisingly quick. After a few feet, Angus came to his first obstacle – a large stone overhang. By stretching his hand across the overhang he located a cloverleaf-shaped air hole, which give him just enough purchase to lever himself up and over. He rapidly ascended the next section and arrived at a further overhang at the bottom of the parapet. Repeating the manoeuvre, he suddenly found himself inside the stone parapet – a sort of decorative crown a good fifteen metres above roof level. From here, he was able to lean over and help first Fanshawe, then Trinculo and finally Jack up and into the parapet.

They made it just in time. Looking across the roof from their position perched up in the shadows, they saw two figures emerge from the darkness.

"Keep down!" Jack whispered.

They crouched behind the low crenellated wall of the parapet. Fanshawe was exhausted. He plonked his bottom onto a narrow part of the parapet. Jack wished he hadn't. There was a loud squawking as a fat pigeon made a brave bid for freedom from Fanshawe's descending buttocks. But Fanshawe was unable to control his downward momentum and the poor bird was flattened.

"Don't move!" Angus hissed.

Below, the two men cautiously approached the eastern turrets, their crossbows at the ready. They tested the locked doors on each of the two turrets in turn. Jack could hear them in furtive discussion and he strained to hear what they were saying. All he could tell was that they were not speaking English. It sounded more like Italian, or... Spanish.

After a further search of the roof, the men crept back over to the open doorway in the north-west tower and disappeared down the staircase. Jack leaned his head on the stonework behind him and let out a long sigh of relief.

Angus whispered, "They've gone. What now?"

"We can't stay up here – we'll freeze to death."

"We should stay here for as long as we can stand it, then maybe drop back down when the service is finishing."

Angus peered down. "I reckon getting down's going to be harder than coming up." He thought for a moment. "I know... give me that."

He took his own backpack, and then Jack's, and fiddled with the straps to tie them together. "Not perfect – but I can probably use this to sort of belay each of you down, across the overhang at least, so you can get a foothold."

As the service finished and people began leaving the chapel way below, they started their descent. Jack went first – initially dangling like a pendulum from the straps of the backpack. He hung in space for a moment and caught sight of the poorly lit street – a good sixty metres below. If Angus let go or if he slipped, he'd have about three seconds to live. At last, his foot touched the safety of a cloverleaf air hole and in a few minutes he had picked his way back down to the safety of the roof. The others followed and soon they were back at the open tower door. All was quiet. Then, as they started on their way back down the spiral staircase, Jack noticed another small wooden door – one they had not seen when they first entered.

"Hey, what's this?" He tried the handle. "It's open. Come on!"

There was no light, but they pressed on regardless, closing the door behind them. They didn't know it, but they were now in the giant attic of King's Chapel, between the roof and the great stone ceiling vaults. The thin layer of stone under their feet was the only thing between them and the vast emptiness of the chapel below.

"Musty in here."

"But it's indoors and safe. I vote we hunker down here till morning and then make our move."

Day of Deliverance

Jack awoke shivering. His whole body ached. The nervous exhaustion from their efforts the night before had somehow carried them through a night of fitful sleep on the cold stone floor. There was now some light in the attic area and he reached over and gently shook the huddled shapes of the others who awoke, groaning.

They retraced their footsteps down the spiral staircase and then crept out of the door at the bottom of the turret and into the chapel. All quiet. Soon they were across the college quad, through the gate and into the street. Jack was tired, cold and aching, but he was also exhilarated by their incredible escape. He banged Angus on the back.

"We made it!"

Wrong. Suddenly, he felt a cold lump of metal pressing against the back of his neck.

A voice whispered, "Do exactly what I say."

Peace, Love and Understanding

They were bundled into a covered cart. One of their assailants travelled in the back with them while the other took the reins at the front. Jack had little time to study the men but he could tell immediately they were not the Spaniards who had pursued them up onto the chapel roof the night before.

The man with the pistol was firm but surprisingly polite. "I apologise for the rough tactics, but you are in great danger. I would like each of you to lie down on the bottom of the cart until we get out of town. We will then have more time to explain."

"But..." Trinculo started to complain. The man, suddenly flushed with anger, thrust the pistol into his face.

"Do what I say," he ordered.

They lay flat on the rough wooden surface of the cart. Although Jack was scared, he noticed that the pistols the man wielded didn't look very sixteenth century – in fact they were bang up to date.

Jack's body was still aching from the night spent up on the tower and being bashed around on the bottom of the cart as they headed out of town didn't help matters. After a while, the driver turned back towards his colleague.

"Here – this'll do."

The cart rumbled to a halt.

"Right, gentlemen, I want you to get up, one by one, and step down from the cart. Please don't try anything stupid."

They had pulled up by a small copse next to the road. The landscape was flat and boggy for miles in every direction and in the distance they could still see the spires of Cambridge. The sun had risen into a clear blue winter's sky and Jack waited for its weak rays to warm his bones.

"Sit down by the wall there."

The men seemed more relaxed now that they were out of Cambridge. They both looked to be in their mid thirties, fit and clean-shaven.

"Here we go."

The taller of the two men handed round a steaming thermos. Fanshawe and Trinculo looked confused.

"What is it?"

The man chuckled. "Not something you will have tasted. We call it tea."

Jack took a sip. As the hot liquid slipped down his throat he began to warm up.

"And this might help..."

The man handed out some dried salt beef. Again, Fanshawe and Trinculo were suspicious, but seeing Angus and Jack help themselves, they tucked in.

"Better?" the man asked. Jack nodded. "First, an apology for the gun toting. We needed to get you out of there quickly. Now... introductions."

"My name is James Whitsun," he gestured to the shorter man, "and my colleague here is Tim Gift."

But Jack had already worked out who they were. "You're Revisionists."

Gift smiled. "And of course you are Jack Christie and Angus Jud." He sighed. "You don't know how much trouble you've caused us."

"So you can explain why those people were trying to kill us and what is going on?"

Whitsun took a slug of tea and a deep breath. "Yes. Your friend Marlowe doesn't just write plays. He has some unusual, and dangerous, friends. He also has an addiction to risk-taking... and money. He seems to have got himself into a position where he is what we would call a double agent. He works for the English state, and also for the Spanish state. Not a particularly comfortable position to be in as the two countries are virtually at war. But he thinks he's cleverer than both."

"Those people who chased us last night, they were Spanish?"

"Correct, Jack. Marlowe is involved in a Spanish plot against the English state. Those men are Spanish agents who are working with Marlowe. Marlowe has all sorts of connections among the aristocracy and the court – he is a useful asset. The Spanish are known to us and we have inveigled our way into their trust. Recently, however, Marlowe has also come to the attention of Sir Francis Walsingham – Secretary of State."

"The founder of England's first secret service," Gift added.

"The Spaniards have been keeping a close eye on Marlowe and saw you accompany him to his rooms. They were suspicious that you might be after him. They may even have thought you were also working for Walsingham. In order to save himself, we understand that Marlowe told the Spaniards that you had threatened him and searched his apartment. He said you had panicked when the Spaniards arrived, and that you then escaped with knowledge of the plot to take to Walsingham in London."

"And they believed that?"

"Marlowe got away with it – he is no fool – and the Spanish will have him safe and secure by now. He betrayed you, but you've been very lucky. Once we became aware of your situation, we were able to distract the Spaniards sufficiently to pick you up."

Fanshawe muttered bitterly, "If I ever see that Marlowe again, I'll..."

Jack interrupted. "So, how do you know these Spaniards? What do you mean they trust you? And how did you find us... rescue us?"

Whitsun glanced nervously at Fanshawe and Trinculo. "A little too much information, for just now, Jack. However, we are going to take you somewhere safe – to someone who can answer all your questions."

"Who?" Angus said.

"Dr Pendelshape, of course."

Jack's heart skipped a beat when he heard the name.

"But first, we need to know, did Marlowe give you anything before he left?"

Fanshawe looked nervously at Jack. Jack nodded. "Tell them, Harry."

"A letter. I swore on my life not to open it. He also gave us money for our services to take it to Walsingham," Fanshawe replied.

"Perfect. If you can hand us the letter, please."

Fanshawe hesitated.

Whitsun insisted, an undercurrent of menace in his voice. "Please."

Fanshawe reached into an inside pocket and handed the letter to Whitsun who whisked it from him. "Very good. We certainly don't want this getting into the wrong hands. We'll take a proper look in a minute."

Gift got to his feet. "And now I'm afraid we have some rather unpleasant business to see to." He removed his pistol from inside his cloak and eyed Fanshawe and Trinculo.

"Jack, Angus, you may want to look away. What we have to do is unfortunate, but necessary."

Jack was incredulous. "Hold on, you're not going to..."

"Don't intervene, Jack, these people already know far too much – their knowledge could wreck our plans."

As Gift spoke, he was unaware of the odd figure approaching a little way down the track. He was perched up on a donkey and wore a grey hooded cloak – a bit like a friar from a monastery. As he reached the group, he dismounted and led the donkey towards them.

Whitsun and Gift were distracted, and Gift surreptitiously reholstered his weapon.

"What now?" he muttered impatiently.

The figure walked slowly towards them, the hood of his cloak covering his head. He did not reveal his face.

"What do you want old man?" Gift said.

"Alms for the poor."

"We have nothing, go away," Whitsun replied in frustration. "We're busy."

"In that case, peace be with you."

Without raising his head, the friar made a sign of the cross in the air. Then, as Whitsun and Gift started to turn away disinterestedly, he placed his hand inside his cloak and withdrew a heavy wooden club. The first blow caught Gift square on the head and he crumpled to the ground. Whitsun reached for his weapon, but he was not quick enough. With his second blow, the friar buried the club into Whitsun's face. He fell to his knees clutching his nose. The friar landed a second blow to Whitsun's head and he too fell unconscious to the ground.

"As I said – peace be with you – brothers."

The friar threw back his hood and his face was revealed.

"Monk!" Fanshawe cried. Immediately Fanshawe and Trinculo embraced their old friend.

"Steady, steady."

"But how...?"

"You didn't think I would let the great Fanshawe Players leave town without me, did you?"

"You followed us?"

"We were thrown out of the buttery late last night. I checked Marlowe's rooms – but he had gone... and so had you. I searched college, but found not a trace. I had to sleep in one of the staircases. This morning, I went out into the street. I saw you come out of King's College and I was about to shout, and then I saw those two men take you. I decided to follow..."

They laughed. "Thank you for that Monk. I didn't know you cared."

Monk shrugged, sheepishly. "You're the only family I have."

Jack knelt down to inspect Whitsun and Gift.

"Are they dead?" Angus asked.

Jack felt for their pulses. "No, but they're out for the count."

"What do we do?"

Jack thought to himself. "They can take us to Pendelshape, but on the other hand, they are completely ruthless. Look what they just tried to do."

Monk wielded his club. "I say we finish them off right now."

Jack put up his hand. "No. You don't want blood on your hands. We'll tie them up nice and tight – that'll give us time to get away. Angus, you help me search them for anything useful."

A moment later, Jack and Angus were rummaging through the clothes and belongings of the two men while Fanshawe, Trinculo and Monk prepared to leave.

Angus removed the two pistols. "We'll take those for a start."

"And I think we'll have Marlowe's letter back," Jack said.

Jack felt a smooth object in one of the inside pockets. He looked round to be sure that the others were busy. "Hey, Angus," he whispered. "How much do you think VIGIL would like to get hold of a Revisionist time phone?"

Angus smiled, slyly, revealing the object he had just recovered from Whitsun.

"Or even two Revisionist time phones."

The Cross Keys

Jack smelled it first: the stench of two hundred thousand people bundled together into a few hundred acres of narrow, fetid streets, slippery with the slime of rubbish. As they walked on, timber and plaster houses rose above them – their upper floors built out over the lower floors so that they almost met at the top. Periodically, refuse was thrown from the windows straight into the gloomy, sunless streets below. You had to take care to avoid a direct hit. Some parts of the streets were little better than open sewers. Despite the overcrowding, there was still room for over a hundred and twenty churches as well as an entire cathedral. Fanshawe mentioned that God had little pity on the residents who were targeted by swindlers, pickpockets, cutpurses, cozeners and countless other forms of low-life. If the undesirables didn't get you, disease probably would. The place was racked with it – bubonic plague, tuberculosis, measles, rickets, scurvy, smallpox and dysentery. Yet despite all this, there wasn't a city to match it in England or even Europe. This was a city destined to become the centre of the largest empire the world had ever seen. A city that was vibrant, bustling and dangerous: London.

For Jack and Angus, it was the smell they found hardest to get used to. Then there was the lack of drinking water. Water was dangerous as it might carry disease. Ale was the next best thing. It was mostly weak but there were stronger brews. That morning at breakfast, Fanshawe had thought nothing of downing two pints of a cloudy liquid with no froth, called 'Mad Dog'. If you didn't like Mad Dog you could try Huffcap, Merry-go-down or Dragon's Milk. Or if you were feeling brave you might prefer Go-by-the-wall or Stride Wide. Not wanting to die of thirst, Jack and Angus had little choice but to try some. Mad Dog was certainly an acquired taste and it was all Jack could do not to retch as the liquid hit the back of his throat. Angus, with his larger frame, coped well with the effects, but after half a pint, Jack's head was spinning.

With the money Marlowe had given him for safe passage of the secret letter, Fanshawe rented a room at the Cross Keys Inn, in Grace Church Street between Bishopsgate and London Bridge. The inn was built around a cobbled courtyard, accessed through an archway from the street. Above the courtyard, open balconies ran round the perimeter of each floor and from here guests could watch plays put on from time to time by itinerant acting troupes. It did seem possible, therefore, that this was a good place to find Marlowe's contact, Wilbur Shake-Shaft, but so far he had proved elusive. Fanshawe's desperation to find a buyer for his plays had caused him to delay the delivery of the precious secret letter from Marlowe to Walsingham. Although he was torn, Fanshawe decided to wait and give a potential rendezvous with Shake-Shaft one more day.

Fanshawe, Trinculo and Monk approached the bar to order lunch, leaving Jack and Angus at one of the wooden tables in a corner of the Cross Keys. Nearby, a log fire was spluttering to life, adding smoke but so far little warmth to the dank air. With the table to themselves Jack and Angus took the chance to review their position.

"Well?" Jack nodded at Angus's doublet under which he hid his time phone.

"Dead as a dodo," Angus replied.

The time phones remained lifeless. There was still no communication from VIGIL or, for that matter, from Tony and Gordon, for whom they were beginning to fear the worst.

"What about the Revisionist time phones?"

"They've got the same problem as VIGIL – intermittent time signals. We have no choice but to wait. We've no other information to go on… we have to wait for a time signal so we can contact VIGIL."

Angus groaned. "Frustrating… we can't communicate with VIGIL, no sign of Tony and Gordon, but if we could get these Revisionist time phones to VIGIL – they would be able to infiltrate the Revisionists and blow their whole operation apart."

"And in the meantime, we're none the wiser about what the Revisionists are really up to. All we know is that it must have something to do with this Spanish plot and that letter to Walsingham."

"Shall we open it?"

"Yeah – I'm thinking it's about time we did. But bear in mind that if we do that, you know, break the seal, then the contents become invalidated. Walsingham might just dismiss it – that's what Fanshawe says."

"Well, at least we've bought some time – you know, with Whitsun and Gift out of the picture." Angus stared down at the table. "Do you think we should have…?"

"What?" Jack asked.

"You know – done the business."

"I'll pretend you didn't say that, Angus. They might be murderers, but we're not. We've got their time phones – so that stuffs them."

"And we've got their guns."

"Yes, but Pendelshape is still at large, and maybe there are other Revisionists with him."

Angus glanced over at the bar where Fanshawe, Trinculo and Monk were involved in an animated conversation with the landlord about their lunch.

"What must they think?"

"They just seem happy to be alive."

"Excuse me." Their conversation was interrupted by a young man who stood at the end of their table. He had an accent that Jack could not place – certainly unlike Fanshawe's. He wore a leather jerkin over a coarse shirt, with long breeches that were tucked into stiff leather boots. He had a mane of long, black curly hair and carried a bag full of papers over his shoulder. In one arm he cradled two large books.

"The landlord left a message for me. He said a Mr Fanshawe was keen to meet and would wait at this table between the hours of eleven and three." He peered at them with dark, glinting eyes. "Is either one of you Mr Fanshawe?"

"No," Jack replied, "but here he comes now." Jack pointed over to where Fanshawe, Trinculo and Monk were navigating their way back through the growing lunchtime crowd, trying not to spill four large pewter tankards of ale. As they arrived, the man held out his hand.

"Mr Harold Fanshawe?"

"Yes."

"I believe you wished to meet me... to do business. My name is Shakespeare. William Shakespeare."

A Bargain with the Bard

Fanshawe was soon well into his sales pitch and papers were strewn over the table in front of them. Unlike Marlowe, and much to Jack's surprise, Shakespeare appeared to be quite interested in Fanshawe's work. He must have been desperate. Maybe it made sense: the great man was as yet unknown, and he would not find fame for years to come. He was looking for anything that might give him a start, an edge. Shakespeare had a nervous energy about him and flicked quickly from page to page. Occasionally he would look up and scratch his beard and make a comment like, "It will need work," or, "This must change," or, "This is wrong."

Fanshawe looked increasingly worried. Finally, he could take no more.

"What say you I read you something... bring the words to life?" He leafed through the sheaf of papers in front of him trying to locate a suitable passage.

"Here!" Fanshawe suddenly jumped to his feet, posed pretentiously and started to speak.

As Fanshawe read out the words, Shakespeare fidgeted with his beard, and stifled a yawn. Jack cringed. Fanshawe's prose was truly dreadful and Jack could sense that, like Marlowe before him, Shakespeare was about to reject the work out of hand. Fanshawe's world was about to implode and, with it, his fantasies of future wealth and fame. But then, much to Jack's surprise, Shakespeare gestured impatiently for Fanshawe to pass him the sheet from which he read. Fanshawe stopped abruptly and sat down, deflated. Shakespeare took the paper and pulled a quill and a miniature pot of ink from his bag, which he placed in front of him on the table. He opened the pot, dabbed the quill and scribbled, murmuring to himself.

"This is wrong… and this… and this would be better here, I think."

After a couple of minutes he had finished and beamed up at them.

"Now Harry, let me see if I understand what you were trying to say."

Shakespeare read out his revised version of Fanshawe's script:

"To-morrow, and to-morrow, and to-morrow,
Creeps in this petty pace from day to day…"

He continued to read, and after a while he paused and looked up from the reworked script. "What do you think?"

Fanshawe stared at Shakespeare in awe. In just two minutes Shakespeare had transformed Fanshawe's efforts. Shakespeare turned to the play's title page: *MacGregor*.

With one final flourish of the quill he struck a line through *MacGregor*, replaced it with *Macbeth* and declared, "Better I think. Also a real Scottish king."

"Yes, sir, much better – more, er, Scottish. You have a gift, sir," Fanshawe said in wonder.

"Yes. I know," Shakespeare replied. "But I usually need something to get me going. A starting point, if you like."

He took a long draught from one of the untouched tankards of ale, thumped it back onto the table and declared, "I'll give you three pounds for the lot."

Fanshawe grimaced. He was hoping for more, but considering the reworking that Shakespeare would need to do, this was a good offer; Fanshawe was unlikely to get a better one.

"Well, sir, I'm not sure…"

Jack cut in. "I don't want to be rude, Harry, but I think Mr Shakespeare is making a good offer… as, er, a friend, I think you will do no better." Then Jack added with a twinkle in his eye, "I assure you – your work could not be in finer hands."

With Jack's endorsement, the deal was done and they looked on as Fanshawe thrust out his hand.

"Three pounds it is, sir!"

"Good. Let's drink to that."

Jack and Angus watched as Fanshawe's papers passed from one side of the table to the other and were stuffed unceremoniously into Shakespeare's bag. Observing the transaction, Jack realised that they had unravelled one of the biggest mysteries of literary history: had Shakespeare written his own material and if not who had? Jack knew Fanshawe's work would give Shakespeare little advantage. But as the great man had said himself – it was a start.

Lunch arrived. Compensating for their meagre rations over the last weeks, Fanshawe, Trinculo and Monk had ordered a vast array of food – different meats, cheeses, cakes and sweet pastries – all of which were delivered together. Lubricated by the arrival of wine and more ale, the conversation turned to the theatre scene in London.

"... and Henslowe has built a new theatre, south of the river. The Rose," said Shakespeare.

"You know this – Henslowe?" Trinculo asked, giving Fanshawe a nudge.

"Of course. I was planning to pay a visit this afternoon."

Fanshawe seized his opportunity. "But William, as you know, we are looking for work. We have many years as players, and young Jack here has a fine talent too. Maybe you could put a good word in for us with this Mr Henslowe."

Shakespeare smiled. "I don't see why not... we can all pay him a visit," he looked at them mischievously, "and after that I have an excellent idea for how we may celebrate the completion of our business."

They turned south down Gracechurch Street. Fanshawe, Trinculo, Monk and Shakespeare were somewhat the worse for wear thanks to the ale and wine they had drunk with their enormous lunch. Progress was further hindered by the appalling traffic. Carts, pulled by two, four or even six horses, moved up and down the paved street. People wove in and out as best they could. As far as Jack could see there were no rules at all – it didn't matter which side you drove down and junctions were a free-for-all – you just moved along as best you could. From the top of Fish Street they caught their first glimpse of the river, a broad expanse of grey-brown water, much wider than it is in modern times. If anything, the river was even busier than the streets. All manner of craft plied along it: small sailing ships, rowing boats, wherries and decorated barges. The traffic moved both up and down the river and to and fro across it, because there was only one bridge: London Bridge.

Initially, Jack had the impression that they were going to cross over the famous structure, but as they drew closer he saw that it was blocked at its north end by an entire flock of sheep. So, instead, they walked down steps to the water's edge where watermen touted for business. Fanshawe pushed forward and soon all six of them were packed precariously into a two-man wherry and were being rowed out into the icy current.

From their vantage point on the river they had an excellent view of the bridge, with its twenty stone arches. A waterwheel had been built into the northern-most arch. On top of the arches, houses were stretched up to six storeys high. Some projected far out across the river, balancing perilously on a system of struts and supports. Teetering towards the southern end there was even a palace – Nonsuch House – complete with turrets, gilded columns and carved galleries. On the far side of the bridge you could make out the high masts of merchant ships waiting to unload at the Custom House.

As they approached the south side of the river, Jack spotted a number of long poles that projected high above a building on the bridge at the southern end. They had strange-looking blobs on the end like giant matchsticks. Jack could not make out what they were at first, but then he realised and felt sick to his stomach. They were heads; the heads of traitors and criminals. A gruesome warning to all who passed beneath and a brutal reminder to Jack and Angus of the reality of the age in which they were stranded.

From the outside, the Rose was a high polygonal structure of timber and plaster – it looked similar to the pictures of the Globe Theatre Jack had seen in books. The place seemed dead, but Fanshawe banged on the door anyway. There was silence. Fanshawe hammered on the door again and shouted, "Anyone at home?"

A voice from inside the building called, "We're closed."

"We want to speak to Philip Henslowe."

"He's busy."

They looked at each other.

Shakespeare spoke. "But we have urgent business with him."

"I told you he's very busy."

"Where?"

"In the pub."

Fanshawe rolled his eyes. "This is hopeless – maybe we should come back later."

Shakespeare's eyes twinkled. "Good idea." He nodded towards a group of people who were gathering nearby. "I know exactly how we can while away a few hours."

Quite close by there was a second building, larger than The Rose. Outside, a large and excited crowd jostled for position. Shakespeare, Fanshawe, Trinculo and Monk pushed in and Jack and Angus followed.

"What's all this?" Angus asked – his face pink with the cold.

"No idea," Jack replied.

Fanshawe paid two pennies for each of them to enter the building and they found themselves standing in a large-roofed gallery overlooking a shallow pit. The place was packed. It was as if there were a giant party going on. People were drinking and eating and there were occasional catcalls and loud whoops of excitement. The arena below looked a bit like a circus ring, but there was no evidence as to what form the entertainment would take. They didn't have to wait long to find out.

First of all a horse was released into the arena. A waistcoated monkey clung on to its back and screeched loudly. Then, four small dogs were released from pens in the perimeter of the pit and they started to chase the horse round and round the arena snapping wildly at its hooves and jumping up at the monkey. The audience wailed with laughter. But Jack could see that the horse was terrified. Occasionally, a dog would manage to clamp its jaws around one of the horse's legs and the poor beast would buck wildly. The monkey would give an ear-piercing screech and hold on even more tightly to avoid toppling off. The horse bucked and kicked again and again until the dog was finally thrown free, whereupon the whole brutal procedure repeated itself. It was a sickening sight, but this was just the beginning.

After several circuits of the arena, the snapping dogs were pulled off and the bloodied horse led away. The mood in the crowd changed to a low chatter of anticipation. Suddenly, there was a crescendo of excitement and people pointed over to one side of the arena. A large bear was being lead forward by two keepers. The great beast moved slowly and seemed to take little interest in the proceedings. The keepers kept prodding it with large sticks to drive it on. The bear had a manacle around one leg, tethering it by a chain to a short post in the middle of the arena. The keepers moved off and for a moment the bear was left to sit quietly, minding its own business. Next a bull was released into the arena. Unlike the bear, it was highly agitated and circled the bear, hoofing the ground and tossing its head. Finally, four large mastiffs were released and, to the crowd's delight, complete mayhem ensued.

The hungry dogs attacked the bull first. One of them was speared by its horns and tossed high up into the air. It landed and did not move. The other mastiffs were not deterred. They circled the bull, occasionally charging and snapping at its legs. Astonishingly, the keepers remained in the ring as the appalling spectacle continued. When the action seemed to subside they would prod one of the dogs with a stick and it would re-enter the fray. After a while, the dogs became less interested in the bull, which was proving a highly resilient adversary, and turned their attention to the bear. They moved towards it – growling and getting closer and closer as they became braver. The mood of the bear transformed. It jumped up onto its hind legs pawing at the dogs and roaring. Suddenly one of the mastiffs came in too close, snapping away with its razor-sharp teeth. The bear got lucky. It grabbed the dog around its trunk, hugged it to its chest and crushed it, before discarding it like a rag doll.

Jack had seen enough.

He turned to Angus. "This is sick, I'm getting out… you coming?"

"I'm right behind you."

It seemed that Fanshawe was also becoming impatient, unlike the rest of the audience who, judging by the delirious shrieks and whoops, were settled in for the afternoon. Fanshawe knew that he had already wasted enough time. His business with Shakespeare complete, he could no longer delay delivery of the precious letter to Walsingham and the generous reward it would bring. He nudged Trinculo to indicate that they were leaving – but Trinculo, Monk and Shakespeare seemed to be engrossed in the proceedings in the bear pit and elected to stay. Thus Jack and Angus's short relationship with William Shakespeare came to an abrupt end and they left the greatest genius of the English language to while away the afternoon watching various animals being mauled to death.

They left the bear-baiting pit and continued west along the river bank. On the other side, they could see St Paul's Cathedral silhouetted against the grey winter sky. Its spire was oddly stunted as a result of damage from a lightning strike years before. In the far distance were the Abbey and Palace of Westminster. Also across the river, but nearer to them, were the palaces of Whitehall and the Savoy along with other dwellings of the nobility. Their gardens extended all the way down to the river and most had water-gates for easy access to the boats.

"The Paris Gardens," Fanshawe announced airily as they entered an open park next to the river. "We will take a boat back across the river from here."

They moved through the gardens and approached the pier, where riverboats and wherries touted for business. A tall man approached them. Jack thought he looked a little out of place compared to the other river men. For a start he had a rich tan. His clothes appeared to be well made and he wore a fine black cloak.

Day of Deliverance

"Gentlemen – please take my boat. Much warmer and more comfortable."

At the back of the boat was a large area enclosed by a canopy, which protected its passengers from the elements.

"Why not?" Fanshawe said. They boarded the boat and sat under the canopy. Outside they could hear two or three other people boarding and a creak of oars as they glided away from the pier.

After a while the tall man ducked beneath the canopy. He was followed by a second man who also had dark skin and a swarthy, powerful frame. He had one badly disfigured eye and a scar that stretched from his forehead, across the side of his eye and down his cheek. There was something oddly familiar about him, but far more worrying was that both men were pointing heavy matchlock pistols at them.

The tall man spoke. "If you make any noise you will die."

Into Thin Air

Their hands were tied behind their backs and hoods placed over their heads. Fanshawe began to sob.

The man repeated his threat. "I said no noise."

It was difficult to tell in which direction they were going, but after twenty minutes, the rocking of the boat stopped. Jack felt a jab in his ribs and then a heavy hand guided him, still blindfolded, from the boat onto some stone steps that rose up from the river. By peering down his nose, Jack could just make out the terrain and avoid stumbling.

"Where are you taking us?" Angus demanded.

Jack heard a dull thud and Angus groaned.

"I said no talking."

They could not have been far from the city, yet, wherever they were, it was oddly quiet. After a few minutes, they entered a building. Despite the hood, Jack could tell that they were in a reasonably large place because there was stone paving beneath his feet, and the sound of their marching footsteps made a slight echo as they were ushered inside. Was this one of the large houses that they had seen from the south bank of the river? They stopped and Jack could hear the men talking among themselves. They were not speaking English and Jack strained to decipher the language. Then he recognised it – Spanish – and the rest of the jigsaw fell into place. Their captors must be the men they had evaded in Cambridge.

He heard a key turn in a lock and they were pushed forward again.

"Down," the man said.

Jack stepped down a stone staircase that led beneath the house. It smelled damp and musty. Without daylight filtering through his hood, everything was completely black. The rope around his wrists was beginning to rub. They reached the bottom of the staircase and

Day of Deliverance

Jack felt himself being manhandled across a room and pushed up against a cold wall. A kind of metal cuff was placed around his ankle and he heard the clanging of a heavy chain. The hood was suddenly ripped from his head. At first he did not understand what he was looking at, but then, as the features of the room slowly came into focus, he felt an overwhelming sense of terror.

All three of them were manacled to a brick wall which formed one side of a large cellar. The only light came from candles flickering in the gloom. Directly in front of them was a rectangular wooden frame, slightly raised from the ground. It had rollers inserted into it and two metal bars at each end. Attached to the bars were looped rope fasteners. There was a large lever on the top bar and this, in turn, linked to a system of chains and pulleys within the structure. With growing horror, Jack realised what the strange machine was: a torture rack. The limbs of its victims were tied to the bars with the rope fasteners. Turning the handle and ratchet attached to the top roller would gradually increase the tension on the chains, which in turn strained the ropes, eventually dislocating the victims' joints. The machine before them was designed to tear its victims limb from limb. The pain would be excruciating.

Fanshawe howled uncontrollably. Without hesitation, the swarthy man with the scar slapped him across his face with the back of his hand.

"Silence!" he said.

Fanshawe's howls degenerated into intermittent sobbing.

"Enough." The tall, well-dressed man stepped forward from the shadows.

He gestured to the rack. "You like our potro? Or if you wish we have the garrucha." He pointed at a beam on the ceiling to which an elaborate pulley-system was attached. On nearby wooden tables there was an array of stone and metal blocks. The torture consisted of suspending a victim from the ceiling with weights tied to their ankles. As they were lifted and dropped, the victim's arms and legs suffered violent pulls and were sometimes dislocated. Fanshawe could not control himself and wailed again. The thug raised his hand and this time it was enough to silence Fanshawe.

"... or maybe the tortura del agua?" Again the man gestured casually to a number of large flagons of water set out on the stone floor.

"Agua." Despite his fear, Jack recognised the word. He tried to remember what it meant. *Water. Waterboarding. He's talking about waterboarding.* He had heard the expression on the TV. It consisted of putting a cloth over the head of the victim, and pouring water over them so that they felt as though they were drowning. It was barbaric.

The tall man spoke good English. He was calm and polite, his manner contrasting with the horror of the instruments in front of them. It somehow made the threat worse.

"You may call me Señor Delgado." He nodded towards the two thugs who glowered back at them. "My friends here are Hegel and Plato. Now, so we are all clear, I do not wish to use any of our special *equipment*. But my friends here, I am afraid, need little encouragement. You understand, of course. So you will help us?" He walked over to Fanshawe, who stood next to Jack, and smiled at him. Then, he reached down inside Fanshawe's doublet. Fanshawe squealed. Delgado pulled out the sealed envelope that Fanshawe had placed there for safe-keeping.

"Finally, we have it." He broke the seal and opened the letter, holding it close to one of the candles. There was an eerie silence as he read.

"As we thought." He placed the letter back on the table.

"You will tell us all you know about this letter. How you got it and what else you know of our plans."

"I don't know anything. I have not even read it," Fanshawe gibbered.

Without hesitation, the man clicked his fingers. Immediately, Plato and Hegel approached, unshackled Fanshawe and dragged him over to the rack. He kicked and screamed as they lowered him onto the evil device. They were much too strong for him and in a second they tied his legs to the lower bar and his arms to the upper bar. Plato put both his hands on the long lever and looked across at his boss. He grinned, eagerly awaiting the signal to continue.

"Wait!" Jack shouted. Delgado wheeled round. "We were given the letter in Cambridge..."

"Quiet!" Delgado spat in frustration. "Marlowe works for us – and he is safe now – he told us what happened. You were going to kill him unless he gave you details of the plot. You forced him to write the letter. We arrived before you could finish your work. You escaped us in Cambridge, but now we have you. You work for Walsingham and you know Walsingham's other spies. We want their names."

"That's rubbish," Angus shouted out furiously. "We were asked to deliver this letter for money. That's all we know."

Anger flashed across Delgado's face. "You lie!" He clicked his fingers and Plato pulled the lever. There was a creaking of rope and wood as the rack strained. Fanshawe screamed.

"Your friend will die there, if I do not have the truth."

"Marlowe's tricked you!" Jack shouted in desperation.

"Before we continue, we search you for more papers."

The man pointed to Hegel who loped over to Angus and pawed at his clothes. Angus writhed, straining against his chains. "Get off!"

Their situation was desperate. They had no information to give. Jack fought his panic and fear, struggling to think clearly, to come up with a way – any way – they could buy some time. Suddenly, out of nowhere, he had an idea. It was a long shot, but...

Jack hissed over at Angus, "Let him – let him search you!"

Angus looked back at Jack, angrily. "What the hell...?"

Jack said firmly, "Let him!"

Hegel reached into Angus's doublet searching for anything that might be valuable or useful. He patted the breast pocket of Angus's under-vest and felt a lump. He looked over at Delgado with a curious leer.

"What is it?"

Hegel wrestled with the fasteners and then slowly removed the slim object from the pocket. It was his time phone.

Hegel held it out to Delgado with a look of confusion. Delgado approached.

"What is that?" he demanded.

Angus looked at Jack with an expression of extreme agitation.

"It's a kind of lucky charm. We have them, er, where we come from," Jack said.

"Is it valuable?"

"Not really – but you can open it."

"Show me."

"You'll have to untie me."

Delgado nodded at Hegel to release Jack's hands – but he remained firmly chained to the wall by his feet. Jack rubbed his wrists which were already raw from chafing on the rope.

"It is a wondrous thing," Hegel said in awe. "Plato – come look at this!"

Plato left Fanshawe tied to the rack and ambled over to where his friends toyed with the time phone.

"It is made of a strange smooth material – like shell."

"Carbon fibre compound, actually," Jack said, under his breath.

"And you say it opens?"

"Yes – you slide that on the side... and... there."

The VIGIL time phone slid open and the three men's faces lit up with wonder as the intricate display and controls were revealed.

"Like a jewel – do you have others?"

Before Jack could say anything, Plato was searching him roughly and quickly located Jack's time phone and the two others – which they had taken from Whitsun and Gift.

"Four!" Hegel exclaimed.

The Spaniards now had all the time phones. Jack had won them a temporary reprieve but then he noticed something else. From inside the first time phone, the yellow bar winked brightly at them. There was a time signal.

"It produces a shimmering light..." Delgado said.

"It must be magic," Plato whispered in wonder.

Jack knew what he needed to do next and he knew he was taking a huge risk. But it was their only option.

"Not magic and not witchcraft – just a plaything. If you like I can show you something else it does. But you need to stand there, all gather round and touch it."

The three other time phones were discarded on a nearby table while the men gingerly placed their fingers on Angus's time phone. "Now, sir, it does a special trick... you see that little button there?"

"This one?" Delgado asked, pointing at one of the small control pads.

"Yes, that one. You have to press it quite hard."

"What will it do?"

"Nothing really, just a little... er... trick of the light."

Delgado pressed the button and Jack closed his eyes and leaned away.

The air around the three men shimmered. Suddenly the gloomy cellar exploded in incandescent white light. When Jack opened his eyes again, the three Spaniards had vanished into thin air.

Jack turned to Angus. "Now, that *is* magic."

An Old Friend

Angus couldn't contain himself. "Get me out of this!" he cried.
Jack was still manacled to the wall but with his hands free he just managed to reach over to Angus beside him and loosen the rope around his wrists sufficiently for Angus to twist them out.

"What about these stupid chains?"

"You've got me there." The heavy iron manacles that still encased their ankles were chained to the wall.

"There should be a key somewhere..."

"Unless it was in our nice Spanish friend's pocket and it's been zapped into hyper-space with him... you do realise what you've done?"

Jack exhaled. "Sorry – it was all I could think of at the time."

Angus's lip curled up in a half smile. "Actually it was pretty cool. Hilarious in fact. What will have happened to them?"

"No idea. Depends on the space–time fix in the time phone. Guess it was still set from when we left – so maybe it will go straight back to the Taurus. Maybe our VIGIL friends back home will have a little surprise when they come face to face with the Spanish Inquisition. Mind you, the phone was not recalibrated before they went, so for all I know they could have ended up on the moon."

"With any luck they've been vaporised. Those guys were something else. I'd love to see their faces. Imagine if the Taurus has zapped them onto the top of the Forth Road Bridge... or the Statue of Liberty or something, by mistake!"

"We've got other things to worry about. We have a time signal – great. So all the time phones should be activated. Which means we could time travel out of here, except for the fact that we're still tied to these stupid chains and the other time phones are over there on the table."

Day of Deliverance

In the excitement, they had forgotten all about Fanshawe, who was still attached to the rack, in the middle of the room. In contrast to a few minutes previously, he was completely silent. He stared gormlessly from his elevated position on the rack at the spot where the three Spaniards had just... disappeared. His jaw hung loosely from his gaping mouth.

"Are you okay, Harry?"

It was as if Fanshawe had not even heard the words. He just kept staring into space.

Jack tried again, louder, "Harry – you okay? Can you free yourself and get us out of these chains?"

Fanshawe blinked. He whispered, "It is a miracle. We are saved..."

"Yeah. Something like that," Angus said.

"But... how...?" Poor old Fanshawe had endured complete sensory overload in the last hour. He had been kidnapped, threatened with torture and then seen three grown men vanish into thin air.

Jack sighed in frustration. "Harry... can you try and work yourself free of that thing and unchain us?"

It was no use. Even if Fanshawe had been in the appropriate mental state, which he wasn't, he was well and truly trussed up.

"What now?" Angus said.

"If VIGIL are doing their job properly, they should also have got a space–time fix on our location and time period through the time phones."

"But the Revisionists' time phones are also activated so they will know where we are too."

"That's if Whitsun and Gift have escaped and reconnected with the Revisionists. Then they'll have told them that we've got their phones, and they won't be happy."

"So we just have to wait and see who gets here first...?" Angus pulled on the chain again in frustration. But it was hopeless. They had got rid of the Spaniards, but they were still stuck.

"What's that?" Jack said, suddenly.

"Footsteps? Upstairs in the house? Someone's here already?"

"But is it VIGIL or the Revisionists?"

"Or some other joker?"

There was an almighty crash as the cellar door was forced open and splinters of wood rained down the stone stairs. Next, they heard someone gingerly making their way down the steps into the cellar. Angus and Jack craned their heads to try and make out the figure, but from their position, chained to the wall, their view was impaired. Suddenly a powerful beam of light shone towards them.

Jack whispered to Angus, "A torch?"

They didn't recognise the figure silhouetted behind the bright light at first.

"Good evening, gentlemen. It looks like I got here just in time." The voice was unmistakable – Dr Pendelshape.

Pendelshape scanned the room quickly to make sure there was no one else there. He then turned his attention to Jack and Angus.

"We don't have much time. We've got to get you out of those chains."

"Yes, but we don't know where the key is."

Pendelshape searched the wooden tabletops. The first things he spotted were the remaining three time phones laid out on one of the tables.

"At least we have those back," he said. "And an extra one... a VIGIL time phone." He smiled. "Now that is going to come in handy." He opened each of them in turn and powered them down. "We don't want anyone else to know where we are just now, do we?"

He quickly looked through the boys' backpacks, that had been left on the floor, and found the two pistols belonging to Whitsun and Gift.

"I think you're still a bit young to be carrying firearms."

Pendelshape picked up the letter from Marlowe that lay, opened, on the table. He read it quickly and nodded. "As we thought – it confirms what we already know." He put the letter back on the table and started looking about for the keys.

"Let's try these." He held up a metal ring with a number of large keys hanging from it and soon Jack and Angus were free.

"I have a carriage waiting outside that can take us to safety."

He paused and looked over at Fanshawe. "But there is one final piece of business I must attend to first."

Pendelshape opened his doublet. Beneath it was a tight-fitting vest, similar to those the boys wore. It had a number of pockets and recesses and Jack noticed that one recess was shaped like a holster. It was from this that Pendelshape pulled out a pistol. He strode matter-of-factly over to where Fanshawe still lay and pointed the gun at his head. The action closely mimicked that of Whitsun and Gift outside Cambridge only a few days before.

"No!" Jack screamed.

Pendelshape swivelled round, a bemused expression on his face. "No?"

"You can't just *kill* him!"

"He's seen too much... he knows too much about the plot. He may upset our plan."

Jack was outraged that Pendelshape, just like his thuggish friends Whitsun and Gift, could contemplate such a barbaric act.

"But, but... he knows nothing. The poor guy has simply been a messenger. He does not know who you are – or who we are for that matter. He is utterly harmless."

Fanshawe, who was still attached to the rack, was slowly regaining his senses.

"I do not know anything of this... *please*..." he begged.

Pendelshape thought for a moment and shrugged. "So be it. I will release you – you have young Jack here to thank – but you must leave this house at once. If you return or speak of any of these events you risk your life. Do you understand?" The decision not to murder Fanshawe was taken as easily as the decision seconds before to kill him. Jack was staggered by Pendelshape's casual disregard for human life. Fanshawe looked at Pendelshape and then back at Jack. Jack nodded. Fanshawe sobbed with relief. Jack had saved his life twice in one day.

They emerged from the cellar into a large kitchen at the back of the house. It was night-time now and they could see only by the light from Pendelshape's torch and a few candles that had been left to burn down. Pendelshape led them to the front door of the house and out into a clear, cold night. It felt good to be out of the dank cellar, breathing the fresh, crisp air. A small carriage waited with its driver a little further down the road.

Pendelshape pointed out Fanshawe's route. "That way – it will take you to the Ludgate Hill eventually. And remember what I told you," he added menacingly.

"Yes, sir. Thank you, sir," Fanshawe answered.

Pendelshape turned to the carriage driver and whispered some instructions.

"Right – you two in there. No funny business. We have a lot of catching up to do."

Jack and Angus had little choice. Fanshawe shook Angus's hand and then glanced towards Pendelshape and the carriage, before putting both his hands over Jack's and looking him in the eye. "Thank you, Jack, for all you have done for me." Then he whispered, "I will repay you."

Pendelshape was getting impatient. "Go!" he boomed out, as Fanshawe scurried off into the night.

Jack, Angus and Pendelshape climbed into the carriage and it rumbled off. Drained by a traumatic day, Jack, and then Angus, fell asleep.

The carriage picked its way up the bumpy road and away from the riverside mansions. An hour after it had melted into the night, two furtive figures appeared at the door of the house that they had just left. After an initial check around the outside, the two men proceeded to break into the house and search it. They found it empty but for the sinister torture equipment secreted in its cellar. If Jack and Angus had left the house only an hour later, they would have met the men and recognised them immediately as Tony and Gordon, their comrades from VIGIL.

The Beautiful Game

"Where are we?" Jack asked. He peered through a small window onto a muddy farmyard. The fields beyond had been dusted white from a light flurry of snow.

"Wembley Stadium," Pendelshape said matter-of-factly as he busied himself at a small wood stove. He was cooking eggs and bacon, and had already managed to produce a pot of very acceptable coffee. He seemed to be completely at home. "Not literally of course. It's where the new Wembley Stadium will be in the future. You're probably sitting exactly where the England team would get changed." He craned his head to view the frozen farmland that stretched into the distance. "As you can see, it's a pretty far cry from the view out there today." He served the eggs and bacon onto three dishes and placed them on the table. Jack was ravenous and the food smelled incredibly good.

Pendelshape had based himself in a farmer's cottage. He had negotiated a generous rent in return for complete privacy for the duration of his stay. The cottage was on two floors – a higgledy-piggledy oak-framed construction. It was quite well appointed. The beds had been dry, and when the fire got going, the house warmed up quickly. In any case, when they had arrived the night before in the carriage, Jack had been so exhausted that he had fallen asleep as soon he had got into bed.

Pendelshape ate slowly, eyeing Jack and Angus thoughtfully from time to time. He had not really changed. Maybe he had shed some weight from his portly frame, but the crow's feet around his deep-set eyes and the cropped grey hair were still the same. The last time Jack had seen Pendelshape was in a First World War trench six months earlier. That was when he showed Jack and Angus the true horrors of war in a final attempt to get them to desert VIGIL and join him and Jack's father. Jack and Angus saw the horrors of war all right – Pendelshape's badly conceived escapade nearly got them killed in the process. It was the final straw for Jack – the moment that finally convinced him that meddling in history was too dangerous, however well planned and well meaning. It was also the moment when he had realised that Pendelshape had a screw loose. Jack had seen him turn from being his affable but eccentric History teacher into a fanatic who would stop at nothing to get his own way.

"So, gentlemen, it would appear that we have some decisions to make." Pendelshape spoke calmly, but Jack could feel the menace in his voice. "Or to be more precise, *you* have some decisions to make. But first of all, I should perhaps explain what you are embroiled in. I have to say that you have been extremely lucky to escape with your lives."

"I think we know that," Angus said, through a mouthful of bacon.

Pendelshape ignored him. "First things first. I am sure you will be pleased to hear that my colleagues, Mr Whitsun and Mr Gift, have recovered. I understand from them that you two had nothing to do with their injuries… which I am glad to hear. They have learned a valuable lesson."

"Where are they?" Jack asked.

"They managed to make it to our rendezvous… somewhat worse for wear, and they have now been deployed elsewhere, ready for the next stage of our plan. We will meet them later."

"What were they doing in Cambridge – and how did they know we were there?"

"The people who kidnapped you were Spanish spies. Marlowe works for them. But what they don't know is that he also works for Walsingham – Queen Elizabeth's spymaster. Marlowe is a double agent. The letter contains details of a plot against the English state."

"What kind of plot?"

Day of Deliverance

"As you know, Jack, this is a dangerous period in history. Phillip II of Spain has finally lost his patience with England. English ships have continued to steal from Spanish ships. Under Elizabeth, England is a Protestant country – Catholics are tolerated, although there is much tension between the two religions. The execution of Mary, Queen of Scots, a few days ago, was the final straw. Mary was implicated in a plot to overthrow Elizabeth and for this she was executed. Killing a fellow monarch is a grave act. The history books tell us that Phillip plans to capture the English throne and finally get rid of Elizabeth. He is mobilising a mighty navy – the Armada."

"Didn't Miss Beattie tell us that that the Armada was defeated?" Angus said.

"It will be. The whole thing is badly conceived, badly planned and badly executed. In addition, the Spanish do not take into account the superior design of English ships, gunnery and tactics. And finally, of course, there is the weather; the storms that finally scatter Phillip's great ships off the coasts of Scotland and Ireland. Half of the Armada's one hundred and thirty ships will be lost or irreparably damaged. England will lose none. The loss of Spanish crew and soldiers will be equally severe. Two-thirds of the Armada's thirty thousand men will die – and for every one killed in battle, another seven will perish by execution or drowning, or die from disease, starvation or thirst."

Pendelshape had a glint in his eye as spoke. It was as if Jack were back in his History class.

"The Armada's attempted attack will end in tragedy. And from that point on, the balance of power in the world will gradually tip in England's favour. The defeat of the Armada is a turning point."

"But why does this concern you? You're not just on another field visit, are you?"

"No, Jack, as I'm quite sure you are aware." He refilled his coffee cup. "Let me show you something."

Pendelshape got to his feet and walked over to a case on the other side of the kitchen. He opened it up, took out a slim laptop and placed it on the table in front of them. The device looked completely out of place in the old kitchen.

"Nice computer, Sir." Angus had not quite lost the habit of calling Pendelshape 'Sir'.

"Indeed. But you won't find this one on the market at home. We've had to make a number of modifications to run our simulation software." He tapped the keyboard. "Now, this should do it. Yes, you can take a look if you like."

Pendelshape swivelled the screen round to allow Jack and Angus a better view. It showed a picture of earth. It looked a bit like Google Earth, except in one corner there were the words 'Timeline Simulator' and in the other the date and time. There were a number of complicated toolbars at the bottom and left of the screen.

"So this is a political representation of the world as it is today, February, 1587. You can see England and Scotland (two different kingdoms, of course), France and the Italian city states. And there is Spain, shaded in yellow. You can already see Spain's influence in the New World – Central and South America – and in other places like the Netherlands. In fact, it is the Spanish army in the Netherlands that Phillip II plans to transport to England, using the Armada to defeat the English. You can see just from the colouring on the map that Spain is a major power, although you don't see the wealth of Spain, which is also huge, because of the stream of gold and especially silver transported from the New World. Anyway, look what happens if I run the simulation forward. I'll do this on the 'Baseline Simulation' – this shows what happens if you don't make any interventions in history as it currently stands."

Pendelshape touched the screen, and the year counter on the right started to count forward the months and the years.

"Cool!" Angus was impressed.

Jack rolled his eyes.

As the years progressed on screen the colours on the map grew and shrank in line with the political influence of the various countries of the world. The yellow of Spain began to shrink. The small red blob that denoted England slowly started to grow. First, it extended to Scotland and then to North America. As the year counter ticked its way through the nineteenth century, the red shading grew across all parts of the world like an infectious disease: India, Australia, Africa – the British Empire. At the same time, the extension of power of the other European nations was shown: blue for France and black for a unified Germany. The counter then moved on through the twentieth century to show the rise of the Soviet Union and the United States and the decline of the old European countries.

"It's like a game," Angus said.

Jack was a little less impressed. "Looks nice – but what does it mean?"

"Jack, this is the Timeline Simulator – or at least a part of it – the full thing is too resource-intensive even for this mighty machine. This software is the key to it all."

"Key to what?"

Pendelshape sighed. "Let me explain. VIGIL and your friends, Inchquin and the Rector refuse to accept that Taurus can be used as a tool for good."

"Yes. And they have a point. We saw what could happen when we went back to the First World War," Jack said.

"You nearly got us all killed, Sir," Angus said bluntly.

"I admit, at that time we thought we had got it right – but we were still not quite there. VIGIL's concern is that by intervening in the past you can trigger changes, however well intentioned, that may have unforeseen consequences in the future."

"Yes and it can be extremely dangerous. Those consequences could lead to worse things happening. Intervening can backfire," Jack said.

"And VIGIL is right up to a point. But this," Pendelshape tapped the laptop with a chubby index finger, "this little chap changes everything. We have developed causal models of history to such a degree that we can show precisely the impact that changes we make in the past will have on the future. We can also evaluate the different scenarios that arise from this. If necessary, we can make subsequent interventions in time to optimise the results. These interventions may also be used to ensure that we can keep the Revisionist team untouched." He smiled, knowingly. "Obviously there are some things in the present we want to keep... ring-fenced, if you like."

Angus finally finished his breakfast. "So what?"

"So what, Angus?" Pendelshape continued, a note of frustration in his voice. "So we can make measurements of our scenarios. We can evaluate changes we make in terms of their impact on economic wealth, political stability, health and a whole range of other things, including, believe it or not, an index of human happiness."

This was too much for Angus. "You've got to be kidding, Sir. You're saying that you can kind of use that computer to say what would happen to the world if you assassinated Hitler and measure how happy everyone would be as a result?"

"Indeed. It sounds strange, I know, but every scenario has up sides and down sides; winners and losers. What we are seeking to do is to find the best overall scenario which optimises human well-being in the long term – and for that matter the well-being of the planet, and, yes, we can't really do the comparison unless we can measure the scenarios. Happiness is one of those measures. All the measures together are called the Utility Index – the UI."

"So you're saying that you've managed to develop the software to a point where you can really run 'what ifs' and measure the impact."

"Yes, Jack, exactly."

Jack lowered his voice. "But Dad didn't agree with your plans, did he?"

Pendelshape sighed, "We had a disagreement with your father. We were keen to use our Taurus with the new Timeline Simulator, but your father refused until he was sure that you were safely removed from VIGIL's control. Their control over you and your father's fear of what they might do to you, should we act, were the main reasons we didn't do anything with the new system. But he also wanted you to join us – he has always wanted you to follow in his footsteps. We became impatient, the arguments became more heated, and eventually..."

"Eventually what?"

"The team and I decided to remove him as leader of the Revisionists. He left of his own accord, however, and we knew he might do something reckless. There was a risk that he would contact VIGIL and tell them of our plans, to avoid them thinking he was still in charge and that this was all his idea. He was worried about you... and your mother. Your presence here confirms that he did indeed warn VIGIL – although why on earth VIGIL decided to send you and Angus back on a mission as important as this, I have no idea."

"It hasn't quite gone according to plan," Angus said sheepishly.

"But you still haven't explained the 'intervention' you plan to make – why you have decided to come back to this point – and what Whitsun and Gift were doing in Cambridge," said Jack.

Pendelshape gazed out of the window, which was starting to mist up from the warmth in the room. He seemed to be weighing something up in his mind – something important. "I suppose it makes no difference now," he said, turning back to the screen. "Let me show you."

He punched the keyboard again and leaned back. "Here. You can see."

The year counter was reset to 1587 and again the days, months and years ticked forward. This time, something strange happened on the map. The yellow, denoting the extent of Spain's geographical and political power did not decline as before. Instead, first England turned yellow and then gradually the whole of South America, North America and Western Europe. As the years on the counter ticked through the nineteenth century some other colours – blue, black, red – did appear on the screen, but they failed to grow. They seemed to be quickly snuffed out by the yellow shading which continued its onward march until, as the year approached 1894, it engulfed almost the entire world.

Jack stared in wonder at the screen. "Spain rules the entire world? Is that what it means?"

"Not quite. Spain conquers England, of course, and in time that gives rise to what becomes an Anglo-Spanish hegemony – the power base eventually moves to the Americas and that becomes a basis for global domination. What we see here starts with Spain, if you like, but over time it morphs into something different and new."

"And that's a good thing?"

"You miss the point. It's a *better* thing. Very high UI – in the long term."

"But doesn't that go against – I don't know – things like people being free to choose who governs them – democracy and all that stuff?"

"There is a place for democracy, in time, and a democratic global state does emerge from this. Eventually. The point is that there are no countries as such. All artificial boundaries are destroyed as the super state develops. At points, of course, as in any historical process, there is brutality and special interests have to be crushed. But you can only achieve stability through strong leadership and control. In the long term, though, what emerges is much better – certainly better than having hundreds of different countries that can't agree on anything and keep fighting each other."

As Jack stared at the map of the world in front of him, entirely shaded in yellow, it dawned on him that the ambition of the Revisionists and of Pendelshape was utterly astonishing. They planned to use the Taurus to rip apart the fabric of history and start again. It was mindblowing. Jack could see that this ability to play God would be hugely seductive – particularly for someone like Pendelshape.

"How will you do it?" he asked.

"To begin with it's very simple. First Spain must defeat England. The new nation that forms from this must then be guided at certain points through the subsequent centuries, with an occasional hand on the tiller from us. The scenario is also modelled to ensure that the Revisionist team and our Taurus are protected. Ring-fenced, if you will."

"How is England defeated?" Angus asked.

"Ideally, we need to make two interventions. Elizabeth must die. This will result in a power vacuum and internal strife in England – civil war, in fact. This first step is desirable, but not completely essential. Secondly, and more importantly, we need the Armada to succeed. The battle of Gravelines during the Armada was a key English victory. If that can be reversed, then the Armada will succeed, laying the way for a successful Spanish invasion. And with a successful Spanish invasion, order will be restored and we can start the next stage of our work."

"So this plot that we stumbled across with Marlowe... I guess that has something to do with part one of your plan – the death of Elizabeth?" Jack commented.

"Indeed. We researched the period to identify a suitable opportunity. We considered the Babington Plot and using Mary, Queen of Scots, but we dismissed the idea. Our plan now is to avoid an obvious successor to maximise a period of internal strife in England before the arrival of the Spanish. Of course this period is rife with espionage. Your Spanish friends from yesterday have a well-developed plan and Whitsun, Gift and myself are here to make sure it goes smoothly, hence their presence in Cambridge. When they discovered that you were in Cambridge too, they had to act quickly to remove you, so you would do nothing to inadvertently…"

"Alter your plans?"

"Yes. But Whitsun and Gift failed, of course, and now your actions in the torture chamber have put everything back. The Spanish assassination cell will shortly discover that three of their colleagues have mysteriously disappeared and they will very likely abandon the plot."

Jack tried to follow Pendelshape's logic. "So now that this has all happened, your next step must be to infiltrate the assassination cell to make sure that the plot still goes ahead. Right?"

"Correct. With Elizabeth dead, stage one is complete."

"How do you, er… they plan to kill her?"

Pendelshape refilled the coffee cups in front of them. "That, my dear boy, would be a little too much information. But it is all set out in the letter that Marlowe gave you. That is why it was important to prevent it reaching Walsingham. Without it, and with Marlowe safely in the hands of the Spanish, Walsingham and the crown are none the wiser…" Pendelshape patted his sides absent-mindedly. "In fact, where did I put the letter?" Jack and Angus looked at each other. "No matter – I will find it in a minute… Anyway, we know all the details of the Spanish plot and it will not take much to get it back on track. Everything is in position."

Jack's head was spinning as he tried to assimilate Pendelshape's words. There was one question that their old teacher had not answered.

"Why are you telling us all this?"

Pendelshape paused before he spoke. "We need to make some decisions. Or to be more precise – *you* do."

Jack's brow furrowed.

"It's your choice really. You can come with me and join the Revisionists – as we suggested before. Your father is right – just like VIGIL we must also seek to train the next generation. The irony of this great power we have – this power to change history – is that we are still mortal. I will not be here for ever. We need to recruit and train new followers to continue our work. They will ensure that the course of history continues to be maintained for the benefit of the human race. Who better than yourselves to start this process? With you on our side, your father, with his great intellectual gifts, will rejoin us and nothing will stop us then. VIGIL will be destroyed and we will change the world and then keep it changed – for good. This is the opportunity before you." His eyes glinted. "To spell it out – I am offering you one final chance."

"And if we don't join you?"

Pendelshape quietly reached into his holster and pulled out the gun they had seen him wield in the cellar. He pointed it across the table at them. "If you choose not to – I'm afraid you leave me with no option. I do not have the same *family* concerns as your father. If you continue to side with VIGIL and meddle in our plans, you must be removed. If and when I see your father again, I will explain, with great sorrow of course, that you were – what's the expression? *Collateral damage*."

He cocked the gun.

"I need your decision, gentlemen."

Appointment at the Palace

Pendelshape held the gun steadily, less than a metre from Jack's face. Jack's heart raced. He had already witnessed the casual attitude that Pendelshape could take to a human life. His whole demeanour would change, bringing a cold, dead look to his eyes. Pendelshape had that look now. Jack had no doubt that he would carry out his threat. The irony was, of course, that Pendelshape was giving the boys exactly the opportunity that Inchquin had hoped for when VIGIL had sent them back. Their mission was to gain Pendelshape's confidence and infiltrate the Revisionists. On the spur of the moment at VIGIL HQ it had seemed like a good idea; but now, faced with the reality, it was frightening and confusing. Without contact with Tony and Gordon, they had no support, no back-up and no way of communicating with VIGIL. But with Pendelshape's pistol hanging menacingly in the air in front of them, it looked like they had no option.

Through the small kitchen window Jack heard a strange noise. It was a sort of muffled jangling. Suddenly, an object appeared outside the window. The object arced slowly from the left side of the window across to the right. As it moved it bobbed up and down. Through the fog of the steamed-up window it was difficult to make out what it actually was. But it was colourful. In fact, it had yellow and red stripes. As far as Jack could discern, for some inexplicable reason, a large jester's hat was flying backwards and forwards outside with no visible means of support. Pendelshape was understandably distracted by the strange apparition. He rubbed the misted window to get a better look.

"What on earth...?"

Suddenly, the small wooden door on the opposite side of the kitchen flew open. Harry Fanshawe stood in the doorway brandishing a full-length musket – he looked almost as scared as Jack and Angus had been feeling. For a moment the musket wobbled uneasily in his hands. Pendelshape swivelled away from the window and jumped to his feet, levelling his gun at Fanshawe. Fanshawe panicked, shut his eyes and pulled the trigger of the mighty blunderbuss. The flintlock slammed down into the breach and there was an odd delay before the powder inside ignited. When it did, it was as if the whole house had been detonated. The musket recoiled so hard it lifted Fanshawe off his feet and threw him nearly two metres back through the kitchen door. Pendelshape screamed as the crude lead shot embedded itself in his thigh. He immediately fell to the ground, clutching his leg with one hand. Somehow he had the presence of mind to retain his grip on the gun and he squeezed the trigger. The bullet flew into the ceiling and a shower of plaster rained into the room.

Before Pendelshape could fire again, Angus heaved the wooden kitchen table on its side and, using it as a shield, he and Jack retreated from the kitchen. Pendelshape squirmed on the floor, but with the boys protected by the screen of wood, he was unable to get a clear aim. He roared in frustration and fired off a volley of shots. The table in Angus's hands jarred violently as each bullet hit; the wood splintered but the bullets did not get through. They reached the door and Angus dropped the table, leaving it as a horizontal barrier across the threshold. They pulled Fanshawe back to his feet and sprinted out of the cottage into the yard, leaving Pendelshape inside, trapped but still armed.

Outside, Trinculo and Monk had the horses ready. Trinculo put away his jester's hat which, with a large stick poked inside, had been the source of Pendelshape's distraction. Jack rode up behind Angus.

"Let's go!" Fanshawe shouted and they galloped off.

But Angus waited. "Are we just going to leave him there?"

"What choice do we have? He's well equipped – he's not going to die."

"That's what I mean, Jack. We could end it all right here."

"He's armed – in case you didn't notice."

"We could burn the cottage down or something."

Jack punched Angus in the back. "You're not serious? He might be mad and he might be okay with going around killing people randomly, but we're not – remember?"

"Yeah, right, sorry. So what then? Try and take him prisoner or something? Remember our mission."

Their conversation was cut short. The front door of the cottage flew open and Pendelshape staggered towards them, zombie-like, brandishing his pistol and firing wildly from a fresh magazine.

"Okay – screw the mission." Angus jabbed his heels into the horse and they shot off down the farm track after Fanshawe and Trinculo.

It took them two hours to travel back into London. They eventually located a small pub in one of the many roads off Eastcheap. As usual, the city was mobbed, and even assuming Pendelshape recovered from the wound that Fanshawe had inflicted, he would never find them there.

"So why did you come back, Harry?" Jack asked as they huddled around a small table at the back of the inn. Fanshawe had ordered bread, cheese and a round of ale. They talked between mouthfuls.

"It's simple, Jack – you saved my life and I could tell that man was trouble. I decided to follow you."

"To the farm?"

"Yes. Late last night I returned to find help and Trinculo and Monk agreed to come with me this morning. We got the musket from the Rose. It is used on stage sometimes. We brought it just in case. But then everything happened so quickly." There was a pause as Fanshawe looked at Jack with a serious expression. "What's going on, Jack? Who are all these people – the Spaniards, those men in Cambridge? And, and... what did you do to those men in the torture cellar?"

Fanshawe, Trinculo and Monk stared at him. There was silence as Jack searched for inspiration. "We are not sure either, Harry, but we seem to have got ourselves caught up in something that we shouldn't have. I think it all started when we met Marlowe. The letter from Marlowe describes a Spanish plot against England. Marlowe is a double agent – he works for the Spanish but also for Walsingham. He betrayed us to save his own skin. They tracked us down to London to stop us giving the letter to Walsingham and uncovering the plot."

Fanshawe looked confused. "But what about – Pendelwright – what did you call him?"

"Pendelshape." Jack had to lie. "We learned that Pendelshape is one of the plotters too. He is a fanatical Catholic. He removed us from the house because it was too dangerous there and was trying to get more information out of us – but we don't understand why he let you go."

"And then..." Fanshawe's eyes opened in wonder. "Your magic orb – how did it make them disappear?"

Jack's imagination was working overtime. "It's a weapon, Harry. Italian – they're always coming up with strange stuff. We got to know a couple of older students from Genoa... when we were at Cambridge... they, er, sold one to us. You know what it's like these days, you need to be able to defend yourself." It was a terrible lie – but it was the best Jack could come up with. Anyway, the truth was far harder to believe.

Fanshawe nodded and took a sip of beer. "Well that's true. But they just *disappeared*..." He stared, unblinking, into space as he recalled the moment.

Jack shrugged. "Sorry, Harry, I can't really explain it – there are more things in heaven and earth and all that..."

"So shouldn't we warn Walsingham?" Trinculo said.

Jack shrugged. "Perhaps we should – but what would we say? We don't really know anything about the plot – who and what it involves – if you think about it," Jack said. "Maybe we've already done enough through our actions to scare off the plotters. And I think there are plots and counter-plots going on all the time – we'd probably just draw more attention to ourselves."

Fanshawe took another long draught of ale and wiped his beard. Suddenly his demeanour changed and he smiled.

"Well at least we have some good news. We nearly forgot to tell

you!" he nudged Trinculo. "My fine friend Trinculo has been busy."
Fanshawe poked Trinculo in the ribs. "Go on then."

"Yes – good news indeed. When you left the bear-baiting yesterday,
Shakespeare, Monk and I went back to the Rose to see if we could
raise Henslowe. We found him!"

Fanshawe interrupted. "But not only that... tell them, Trinculo!"

"I'm trying to..."

"It would seem that Henslowe has a problem," Fanshawe
continued enthusiastically.

Trinculo was getting annoyed by Fanshawe's interruptions. "He
needs help."

Fanshawe could contain himself no longer. "Yes! Three of his
actors are ill. Very ill. Isn't that marvellous? They want us to replace
them – well, at least temporarily. With any luck they won't recover.
But more than that..."

"It gets better?"

"Much better. Henslowe is in a panic because in only two days'
time his players will be performing at Hampton Court Palace."
Fanshawe was beaming from ear to ear. "It is most excellently
providential."

"Hampton Court Palace – who is he performing for?" Jack asked.

"The queen herself, of course," Fanshawe replied.

Making an Entrance

"**N**o! No! No!" For about the fifth time that morning, Thomas Kyd stormed on stage at The Rose theatre and advanced towards the troupe of actors. Kyd was proving to be demanding, irascible and fussy. Perhaps it was fair enough. In two days' time they would perform his play in front of the queen, her senior ministers and a good section of the court at Hampton Court Palace. It would be the most important day of Kyd's life and in the lives of the Henslowe Players. Nevertheless everyone had just about had enough, including the pompous Edward Alleyn who, being the most famous actor of the day, was not used to being bossed around.

Jack and Angus sat at the rear of the stage under the wooden balcony. Inside, The Rose was like a smaller version of the bear-baiting pit, but in place of a large open arena, the theatre housed a wooden stage, raised about one metre off the ground, which projected out into the middle of the standing area. The stage and standing area were ringed by two levels of roofed wooden galleries. The stage itself was given some protection by a raised balcony and large awning at the rear. Otherwise, the theatre was open to the elements. There was rubbish strewn everywhere and the whole place smelled dreadful.

Fanshawe and Trinculo had hit the jackpot winning parts for themselves in the prestigious play though they had Shakespeare to thank for their good fortune. He, of course, knew Henslowe, who had built the theatre, and was also well acquainted with the famous actor, Edward Alleyn, and the playwright, Thomas Kyd. With three actors taken ill so suddenly, Henslowe and Kyd had been desperate. The stakes could not have been higher. The date at Hampton Court in front of

the queen would be the inaugural performance of his masterpiece –
The Spanish Tragedy.

There had only been one problem – and for this reason Angus had
not stopped smiling since they had been allotted their parts.
Unsurprisingly, there was no role for him – but it did not matter, as
an extra pair of hands backstage was welcome. Jack was another
matter altogether. The only trouble was that the actor Jack was
replacing had been a boy who must have been a little younger than
him and the role was Isabella, the wife of Don Hieronimo. The roles
of women were played by boys or men and, for this reason, Jack was
sitting next to Angus wearing a dress. Jack was not impressed.

"Shut it," Jack said for the umpteenth time that morning. "I have
to learn these words by tomorrow."

Angus laughed. "The things we do for VIGIL, eh? Don't worry, I think
you look really nice."

Jack ignored him.

After a while, Angus lost interest in baiting Jack and pointed over
at Kyd, who was still remonstrating with Alleyn. "They're still at it,"
he said.

Jack glanced up from the script. "Well they better get it
sorted – we haven't got much more time."

Jack and Angus sat in silence. Since their escape from
Pendelshape, both of them had been particularly watchful. For about
the tenth time, Angus said, "No time phones, no contact with VIGIL,
so we just wait?"

"Yes. At least we're safe."

"You think?"

"Safe as anywhere."

"Well I hope you're right." He nudged Jack. "Oh – here we go,
looks like you're on… don't trip over your dress."

Jack got to his feet. "You're hilarious."

The rehearsal finally finished and that afternoon the Henslowe Players
prepared for their departure to Hampton Court Palace early the
following morning. Hampton Court was upstream so the decision had

been taken to transport them up the Thames on two boats. However, as they discovered the next morning, the two tilt boats that had been hired for the purpose were far too small to accommodate the entire cast of *The Spanish Tragedy*, their costumes, props and various hangers on – let alone the overgrown egos of Henslowe, Alleyn and Kyd. Nevertheless, constrained by the limited budget set by Henslowe, who kept a beady eye on all costs, the boats were going to have to do. Fortunately, the weather remained fine and the river was as smooth as a billiard table. Everyone was extremely glad to leave the rehearsals at The Rose and the endless differences of artistic opinion between Kyd and Alleyn.

There was lively chatter as everyone boarded the boats, which rapidly became over-burdened. The river journey would take them slowly up river, past Whitehall and then eventually to Richmond and Kingston beyond. They would disembark a little after Kingston and lodge at the magnificent Hampton Court Palace, where the queen and her entourage were in temporary residence. The following afternoon they would stage the inaugural performance of *The Spanish Tragedy*. With luck, this single performance would seal their fame and fortune forever. Everyone was very excited.

They were all squashed together like sardines in the front boat and the rowers made slow progress. They passed Lambeth Palace on the left of the river and on the opposite bank, Westminster Abbey. As they made their way slowly upstream, the scenes on each side of the riverbank became more rural with the boatyards and villages increasingly punctuated with open fields, farmsteads and woodland.

Jack reflected again on the events of the evening before. Their arrival had saved the day and as a result they had made themselves instantly popular among the Henslowe Players. The group seemed amused by Jack and Angus's strange accents and language, but it didn't bother them – they were used to mixing with and performing in front of all sorts of people. There were about twenty actors in the group but, even so, a number of them would need to double up on parts for *The Spanish Tragedy*. They were all friendly and welcoming – although there was one, Christo, who seemed a little quieter than the others. Perhaps he only seemed that way because all the others, by contrast, were excessively loud.

After a boisterous dinner, they had slept in claustrophobic accommodation next to The Rose, provided by Henslowe (for a fee). There was not room for all of them in the main dormitory and Jack had ended up in a small alcove next to Christo. The actor had been furtive and uncommunicative and, with the conditions cold and uncomfortable, Jack had struggled to sleep. After a while, presumably assuming Jack was asleep, Christo had got out of his makeshift bed on the floor. He had lit a small candle and removed a heavy, ornate cross from his neck and then held a Bible in front of him. He prayed and chanted for what seemed an eternity. Even though Christo's voice had been quiet, his words were uttered with passion. Jack could not make out what he said but he recognised the language. Most of it was in Latin but some of it was in Spanish.

Their last stop before Hampton Court was at Kingston where they took a leisurely mid-afternoon lunch at The Swan before reboarding for the final stretch. The landlord of The Swan was delighted to see them all. A log fire crackled away in a large inglenook at one end of the pub. After nearly a day on the river it was a welcome sight. Soon Henslowe and Alleyn were ordering food and drink and everyone was settling down.

"I'm bursting – where do you think the luxurious facilities are?" Angus asked Jack. They had become accustomed to limiting trips to the loo – firstly because there usually wasn't one anyway and secondly, if there was, the experience was too awful to imagine.

"No doubt a hole in the ground round the back somewhere. Be sure to take your gas mask."

Angus wrapped himself back up in his cloak and disappeared outside again. The Swan was located at the upstream end of the town of Kingston and at the back of the inn was a large yard that led onto a road, partly shielded by some large oak trees. The yard was home to three goats and a number of hens that pecked at invisible specks in the mud. Towards one side, a narrow platform was built over a stream that ran into the river. The structure supported three crude wooden huts. The set-up was luxurious compared to what Angus had experienced in London and he hurried over. The first hut was not occupied and he went in, trying not to touch, smell or look at anything.

As he made his way back to the pub, he saw a carriage with two horses pull up just outside the gates to the yard. At the same time he spotted Christo emerge from the inn and scurry across the yard towards the carriage. The door of the carriage opened and a cloaked figure stepped down to meet Christo. The figure used a walking stick and was limping. Angus recognised him immediately: Pendelshape.

Angus dived behind a pile of logs. From his position he could just spy Christo in deep discussion with Pendelshape. From time to time Christo would glance back furtively at the inn. In less than two minutes the conversation was over. Pendelshape hauled himself back into the coach and it rumbled off.

Angus waited behind the logs until the carriage had disappeared and Christo had gone back inside. When he returned to the pub, the late lunch was in full swing and, encouraged by the landlord, Alleyn, Fanshawe and the rest of the Henslowe Players were taking it in turns to make speeches, sing songs or recite poetry to a growing crowd of onlookers. Christo returned to his place by one of the windows and nibbled at his food. He took little interest in the revelry of his colleagues. Angus sidled over to Jack who had moved next to the fire and was watching and applauding along with the rest of the group.

"Find it?" Jack said.

"Yes, and that's not all I found."

"Really?"

Angus whispered out of the corner of his mouth, "Pendelshape was just here."

Jack gasped. "What?"

"Shhh." Angus looked around the inn, checking out Christo in particular. "Yeah. But he's gone. Don't look now, but he met *him*." Angus nodded at Christo who was ignoring the fun and games in the inn completely and staring thoughtfully out of the window.

"Pendelshape met Christo... and then just left?" Jack whispered in amazement. "But... he might have seen us... he might know we're here."

"Don't think so. It looked as if they'd planned the meeting. As if Pendelshape knew that the troupe would be stopping here. And I kept an eye on Christo – he hardly seems to have noticed us, so I don't think he said anything to Pendelshape."

"Well that's a relief. Close call though." Jack bit his lip. "But what's he up to?"

"No idea."

"I didn't tell you – last night – when we were freezing our butts off in that pigsty that Henslowe put us up in..."

"Least you only had to share with one... I had to share with about ten of them."

"I couldn't get to sleep. Christo didn't realise I was awake – he was praying and chanting and all sorts."

"So? Maybe he couldn't sleep either – don't blame him with the amount of snoring and farting going on."

"Yeah – but he's a Catholic. Not that unusual in itself – but I heard him saying stuff to himself – *in Spanish.*"

"So?"

"Come on, Angus – keep up. A Spanish Catholic in the Henslowe Players has just had a secret meeting with Pendelshape..." Jack said slowly. "And we know Pendelshape wants to use an existing plot to kill the queen and create civil war in England – so the country will be ripe for invasion."

"So you're saying that maybe *this* is the plot – Christo is somehow part of it?"

"Exactly. He's using the Henslowe Players as a cover. I still don't get it, though. The queen is surrounded by bodyguards and soldiers. Even if he was some sort of fanatical killer, I can't see how he would do it on his own."

"Maybe Pendelshape has already worked out some way to help him when we get to the palace, you know, some sort of trap."

Jack stared into the fire. "Yeah – you could be right..."

Word had got out about the arrival of the Henslowe Players and the spontaneous party at The Swan had drawn an enthusiastic crowd of locals seeking to enjoy the impromptu entertainment. Unfortunately, the quality of the performances was declining rapidly as the players became increasingly inebriated. Nevertheless, the landlord was so delighted with his takings and the promise from Henslowe that they would stop off on their return trip from the palace, that he gave the group an entire barrel of Mad Dog and, unbelievably, a live pig.

They tottered back down the pier to the waiting boats significantly the worse for wear. If anything, the boats seemed even more cramped and top heavy than before – particularly the front one, which now carried the barrel of ale and the pig. The pig squealed noisily as it was manhandled aboard and tethered between two of the posts that held up the awning. A large crowd of people from The Swan had gathered to see them off, and with a great cheer ringing in their ears they cast off into the river for the final haul up to Hampton Court.

It only took three minutes before the barrel of Mad Dog had been cracked open and the first round distributed in large earthenware tumblers. Five minutes later the singing started and a mere twenty minutes after that there was the first man overboard. This caused enormous hilarity. It did not seem to occur to anyone that, with the water temperature hovering not far above zero, the man was lucky to be pulled out alive. He didn't seem to care – a dry cloak and a fresh mug of Mad Dog helped him forget the experience altogether. At the back of the boat, even the pig was offered a mug of beer to stop it squealing. It showed its disdain by squealing louder than ever and then promptly defecating – mostly on Alleyn's shoes. Kyd and Henslowe nearly fell out of the boat themselves, such was their mirth. The whole thing was getting horribly out of control. The boat zigzagged its way unsteadily up the Kingston Reach, narrowly avoiding a range of other craft, royal swans and sundry river life.

The sun was beginning to set as they made their final approach and immense bands of purple and pink clouds swooped across the darkening sky. To their right, the great royal deer park stretched endlessly into the distance, and Jack caught occasional glimpses of deer in the dark shadows between the ancient oaks. A low mist was forming on the river and, in the distance, Jack saw the great palace of Hampton Court emerge. Its pink brick had turned a deep crimson in the fading light and from one of its towers Jack noticed the same royal standard that had been flying at Fotheringhay – the quadrants of the fleurs-de-lis and the three lions. But Fotheringhay Castle had been quite different from this. It was a brutal bulwark of stone built for an earlier, more violent age. By contrast, Hampton Court had a gentler façade – its crenellations and towers were there for show and not for defence. It was a palace and not a castle. A palace fit for a queen.

They drew closer and the splendid building loomed above them, its presence quelling the drunken blathering. A small group of men scurried from the bank to the pier to help tether the boats. To mark their arrival, Henslowe, in the front boat, was to give a speech of welcome that had been specially penned by Kyd for the occasion. Although the pig had calmed down a little, it had still found the whole experience highly stressful and the first priority was to lead it ashore. As the boat glided into its mooring, Henslowe took up position at the bow, standing just behind the little flag, emblazoned with the interlinking P and H of his name, which had been nailed to the prow. The afternoon's revelry had taken its toll on Henslowe, as it had with the rest of the troupe, and he swayed uneasily on his feet. He held up the paper with his address of thanks to the bemused welcoming party who looked on from the landing pier. Clearing his throat, he began to speak.

"On this day..."

But at that moment, from the stern of the boat, the pig squealed hysterically as it was finally released. Sensing freedom, it scrambled across the baggage and past the passengers at high speed. It then leaped like a large pink missile from the bow of the boat towards the landing stage. Henslowe had no chance. One moment he was there, the next he was flying through the air, dislodged from his precarious position by one hundred kilos of airborne bacon. The pig hit the landing stage gracefully and slalomed expertly through the surprised onlookers, never to be seen again. Henslowe was not so lucky. He landed in the river with a stylish bellyflop. Everyone in the boat raced to one side to check on the fate of their esteemed leader. The boat was already dangerously top heavy and the whole thing slewed to one side, unbalancing, before it completely capsized. The Henslowe Players, their baggage and the barrel of Mad Dog (now empty) were all deposited unceremoniously into the Thames.

They had made an entrance at Hampton Court, though perhaps not quite as Henslowe had intended.

Hampton Court

The recriminations lasted well into the night and Alleyn, when accused of deliberately releasing the pig at just the wrong moment, had nearly walked out in a rage. By the morning, however, tempers had improved. Luckily the main props had been fished successfully from the river and the costumes were finally starting to dry out. The performance was to start at two o'clock that afternoon, and Jack was surprised and impressed by how professionally the Henslowe Players focused on the job at hand.

Their spirits were lifted further when they were led from their quarters through the great courtyards to the magnificent Great Hall at the heart of the palace where they would be performing. The hall must have been over thirty metres long and twenty metres high and had a splendid hammer-beam roof. At one end there was a finely carved minstrel's gallery and all around were stained-glass windows and magnificent tapestries. In the oriel window to the right of the dais were the arms of Cardinal Wolsey, the founder of the palace, and in the side windows were the badges and devices of Henry VIII and his wives. At the front and down two sides of the hall a number of cushioned chairs had been laid out in three rows. In the middle, at the front, a throne had been carefully positioned from which the queen herself would enjoy the first performance of *The Spanish Tragedy*. A low stage had been erected in the centre of the hall, and towards the rear, a screen stretched from side to side, masking the actors when they were not performing. Angus, his duties as stage hand complete, would be allowed to watch the play up in the minstrel's gallery.

Two o'clock was approaching fast and the cast members were limbering up in earnest. The Great Hall was soon a hive of activity. Henslowe manned one of the entrances, watching nervously for the arrival of the first members of the audience. Kyd fussed from one actor to the next, tweaking costumes and proffering needless advice. Alleyn paced up and down at the far end of the hall in deep concentration, reciting his words to himself over and over again. Even Jack, with his keen memory, had struggled to learn his words in the short time allowed. Much of the script was still in Kyd's own extravagant italic handwriting, which was difficult to read. In addition, a number of the spellings and pronunciations were very odd. It had taken Jack a long time just to work out how Kyd had formed certain letters like 'f' and 's'; he frequently used two or three different sorts of squiggle to denote the same letter. To complicate matters further, there were whole words Jack just did not know or understand. He could recognise the script as English – but only just. Jack was glad he only had one small part to learn.

While Fanshawe and his entourage prepared for the performance, Angus spent the morning lumbering around with the costumes and props. At last everything seemed to be ready and he sat down next to Jack in one corner of the hall for a final breather before the big performance.

"You ready, then?" he asked.

"Think so."

Jack nodded in the direction of Christo on the other side of the hall. "You been keeping an eye on him?"

Christo fiddled with the cross around his neck. If anything, he had become even more nervous as the time of the performance approached. Other than Jack and Angus no one would have noticed – they were all too busy – and anyway it was normal to look nervous before performing in front of the Queen of England.

"Yes, I swear he's getting more jittery," Angus said.

"I think so too and I don't like it. He's got to be planning something."

"Seems like it, I know – but what? We were all searched. And anyway, he would never get away with it – have you seen the number of guards around the place?"

"Well, we know he's up to something and we know that

SPANISH TRAGE-
die, Containing the lamentable
end of *Don Horatio*, and *Bel-imperia*:
with the pittifull death of
olde *Hieronimo*.

Newly corrected and amended of such grosse faults as
passed in the first impression.

AT LONDON
Printed by *Edward Allde*, for
Edward White.

Sixteenth-century illustration from 'The Spanish Tragedy'

Pendelshape can't be far away… or Whitsun and Gift, for that matter. We need to be ready, just…"

At that moment, their conversation was cut short as the large double doors at the rear of the hall flew open. Henslowe had been manning the wrong entrance and missed his big chance to thrust himself in front of the queen. She swept into the Great Hall surrounded by a large entourage of extravagantly dressed men and women. Her stunning white gown was embroidered with gold and decorated with precious stones. Around her neck there was a large lace ruff and her hair was crowned with a ring of bulbous pearls. She had arrived unexpectedly early and walked straight through the backstage area. It took the cast completely by surprise. But she didn't seem bothered. She marched on, nodding in acknowledgement as everyone turned and bowed.

Soon the Great Hall was packed with other members of her court and by the time the queen took her position on the throne, every chair was filled. There was a buzz of excitement. This was it. Backstage, Kyd gave a final pep talk as the actors prepared for the performance of their lives. The first public performance of *The Spanish Tragedy* began.

It went well. The audience applauded generously and, backstage, Henslowe and Kyd were quietly effusive in their praise. Much to his relief, Jack had also performed his part to everyone's satisfaction. They needn't have worried about Christo, either. He was flawless and word perfect. After a short intermission, the second part of the play began and possibly for the first time on their mad adventure, Jack felt himself relax. He stared up at the extraordinary workmanship of the ceiling of the Great Hall above and the opulence of his surroundings. On the other side of the curtain, the Henslowe Players were starting the second act. Jack could hardly believe he had just performed in front of Queen Elizabeth I. The whole thing was utterly extraordinary.

He picked up the script and flicked forward to recheck his words for his final short appearance later on in the play. He had done well so far, and he didn't want to let the side down. As he thumbed through the pages, Kyd's italic script flicked passed his eyes. Suddenly, one of the pages caught his eye. With a jolt like an electric shock, finally, he understood how Christo planned to assassinate the Queen of England.

A Confusion of Queens

The sword fight, just like the one in *Hamlet*, had already started and Christo and Alleyn were battling it out onstage in front of an enthralled audience. Jack poked his head around the curtain. Nobody noticed – they were absorbed by the clanging of swords and acrobatics of the two combatants.

Christo jabbed his sword forward. Alleyn jumped back, but the blade pierced his flesh and instantly an ominous red patch appeared on his billowing shirt. Alleyn glanced down at the wound and looked back up at his opponent, an expression of rage on his face. A frisson of excitement rippled through the crowd. *The Spanish Tragedy* was proving more thrilling than they could have possibly wished.

Christo's strike had found its mark but had unbalanced him momentarily and Alleyn came back with a violent counter-thrust. His blade flashed and caught Christo in the ribs. There was a gasp from the crowd. Sensing his chance, Alleyn darted forward a second time, his sword aimed at Christo's chest. This time Christo spotted the move and swayed to one side, narrowly avoiding the thrust. Alleyn's forward momentum now presented Christo with an opportunity. He grabbed his opponent by the arm and heaved him onwards while simultaneously thrusting out his leg. Alleyn tripped over Christo's extended leg and spun through the air hitting the makeshift stage with a thud, his sword spinning from his hand as he landed. Christo pounced onto his opponent and they became locked in a deadly struggle. But Alleyn was strong and, like a child with a rag doll, he soon had Christo pinned on his back beneath him. Alleyn grasped Christo's sword hand and banged it hard on the ground until Christo relinquished his grip. Christo was nailed to the ground. He was badly wounded and he had no weapon. Alleyn's bulk was pressing down on him and he could feel his life slowly draining away. But it wasn't over yet. Christo gritted his teeth, and with a final super-human effort he jerked his knee upwards into Alleyn's crotch. Alleyn wailed and Christo seized the moment to wriggle free. He snatched up a sword and wheeled round. Alleyn jumped back to his feet and grabbed the other sword and the two of them circled round and round, panting at each other like cornered animals. The crowd jeered. Christo's remaining energy was melting away – he knew he only had seconds left. There was blood all over the floor and Alleyn slipped. He was only distracted for a split second but it was enough. Christo leaped forward to land a second, fatal blow. Alleyn screamed as blood from the wound spurted from his chest. He dropped to one knee, and looked up at Christo before he slumped to the stage floor. Spontaneously, the audience burst into applause.

But the script was about to change.

Jack saw his worst fear unfold in front of him. Christo stepped over the prostrate body of Alleyn in the middle of the stage and marched menacingly towards the queen, who sat on her throne, enthralled by the spectacle before her. By the time the guards, or the queen for that matter, realised that Christo's advance was not part of the play, it would be too late. From his position on the other side of the stage, Jack could do nothing. Christo was only ten paces away from the queen and brandished his sword above his head. There was a ripple of unease in the crowd, then Christo dashed forward. Jack screamed out but it was too late. The point of Christo's blade was only centimetres from the queen's throat. She was about to die. But, suddenly, Christo simply collapsed. He hit the ground like a sack of potatoes right at the queen's feet. It was as if he had been shot through the head by a sniper.

It was the next best thing. Up in the minstrel's gallery, Angus stood staring down at the scene before him. His catapult hung loosely in one hand. From twenty metres away he had unleashed a missile that had cracked into the back of Christo's head, instantly knocking him unconscious.

A Confusion of Queens

The queen was quickly surrounded by four burly guards brandishing halberds. A number of courtiers drew swords and dragged Christo away. But it wasn't over.

Above them, there was a loud shattering of glass as first one, then a second, of the large windows were smashed open. Shards of glass rained into the Great Hall – and Jack narrowly avoided being impaled. At first it was not apparent what had caused the windows to shatter. Then ropes were flung through both windows and two figures abseiled down onto the floor of the Great Hall. They touched down and took up position in the centre of the hall where, moments before, Christo and Alleyn had staged their fight. The two men were in sixteenth-century dress, but Jack recognised them immediately: Whitsun and Gift – their Revisionist friends. Both men were holding something close at their sides, hidden by their cloaks. Jack guessed that they must be automatic weapons of some sort. He was so astonished by the arrival of the gatecrashers, that he did not really notice the strange reaction of the audience. While members of the cast scurried for cover, the audience were oddly quiet and watchful.

Then Jack witnessed something extraordinary. Before Whitsun or Gift could act or speak, the audience all around the hall dropped to their knees – almost as one. It was a perfectly synchronised movement. A few courtiers, possibly ten or fifteen of them, dotted within the audience, remained standing. They were armed with stubby crossbows which, until that point, had been carefully hidden.

Whitsun and Gift had no chance. Without warning, the armed courtiers fired. In a moment, the air was thick with deadly crossbow bolts zipping across the hall. Jack watched as the lethal missiles struck home. Whitsun and Gift were peppered. As he dropped to the floor on his knees, Whitsun searched for the trigger of his gun, but a final bolt skewered his neck and he slumped to the ground. Gift was already prostrate – lying in a growing pool of his own blood, a series of bolts buried up to their feathers in his torso.

The armed courtiers reloaded and stepped forward to take up strategic positions around the hall. Some scanned the windows above, perhaps waiting for more armed raiders; others covered the entrances to the Great Hall. Two of them moved towards Whitsun and Gift who lay centre stage – their lifeless eyes pointed towards the ceiling of the hall. They leaned down to search and check the bodies. Jack recognised the two courtiers immediately: Tony and Gordon. They had somehow inveigled their way into the team of armed courtiers who had sprung the trap for Whitsun and Gift.

A door flew open at the front of the hall and in marched a tall, thin, pale-faced man with a moustache and beard. He was slightly balding and his dark hair was flecked with grey. He had dark, almost black eyes, and was dressed entirely in black, except for a stiff, white ruff around his neck. Next to him walked a woman who was dressed almost identically to the queen. The woman sitting on the throne now stood up to curtsy. It was very hard to tell the two women apart. Jack's head was spinning – Whitsun and Gift dead, Tony and Gordon here... and now, *two queens*?

As the second queen entered the Great Hall everyone turned towards her and bowed. She approached her strange twin and paused briefly. It was uncanny seeing the two women together.

"Lady Sarah, I thank you for your services today," she offered her twin a hand, "your bravery will be rewarded."

The real queen strode forward to inspect the figures of Whitsun and Gift in the middle of the hall. She gave one of them a contemptuous poke with her foot. Tony and Gordon stood nearby, their heads bowed. The hall fell quiet as the queen prepared to speak, her dark eyes glinting with fiery confidence – a confidence wrought from twenty-nine years of hard-earned power. She spoke clearly and defiantly.

"My friends. We have defeated a plot to murder your queen – the Queen of England. Let tyrants fear. I have always so behaved myself that under God I have placed my chiefest strength and safeguard in the loyal hearts and goodwill of my subjects; and I thank you for your help in crushing this foul plot. I know I have the body of a weak and feeble woman but I have the heart and stomach of a king, and of a king of England too, and think foul scorn that Parma or Spain or any prince of Europe, should dare to invade the borders of my realms..."

A Confusion of Queens

The speech continued in a similar vein for some minutes and when it ended there was a great roar of approval and, spontaneously, a chant of "God save the queen!" rang out. She stood, chin high, imperious and triumphant. It took several minutes for the adulation to die down. The queen turned to the dark-clothed man and said quietly, "Walsingham – I trust you will deal with matters now." With that she marched from the hall, surrounded by an escort and followed by her twin – Lady Sarah.

Walsingham took charge. He pointed down at Christo. "The Spaniard – put him in chains. He will be tortured until we know the identities of all the other plotters." He pointed at the bodies of Whitsun and Gift, addressing Tony and Gordon. "Make sure they are stripped and find any other evidence. I have a good mind to send their heads to the Spanish court. And, now, where are they?"

Walsingham looked around the hall. Angus had come down from his position in the minstrel's gallery and was standing with Jack and the other members of the cast, who huddled together in one corner of the stage, agog at the events unfolding in front of them. Walsingham strode over to them. He was a commanding, sinister figure. Tony and Gordon followed close behind. Walsingham eyed the cast of the Henslowe Players and turned his attention to Angus and Jack at the front.

"And you claim that, apart from the Spaniard, Christo, the Henslowe Players had no knowledge of the plot?"

Tony looked at Jack. "Absolutely not. This is confirmed in Marlowe's letter. By waiting and laying the trap here at Hampton Court we knew we would catch any other plotters red-handed."

Walsingham nodded. "Your point is fair." Then he turned angrily towards Angus. "But you… smuggling a weapon into the palace…"

Jack intervened before Angus could answer. "Sir, a theatrical prop – just like the swords." As he spoke, Jack spotted a knowing smile of approval cross Tony's lips.

"Indeed, sir," Tony continued, "the fact that this young man saw the danger of Christo and acted to save the woman he thought to be the queen proves that he had no knowledge of the plot… or indeed the trap we had laid for the plotters."

Day of Deliverance

Walsingham stared at Jack and then back at Angus with beady, black eyes. Jack could almost hear the mind of the queen's spymaster whirring away, carefully analysing their statement for flaws. But in Jack Christie, Sir Francis Walsingham had met a worthy match and at last, Walsingham gave a firm nod.

"Fine. Indeed, more than fine. You and your friends shall be rewarded." His face relaxed – but there was still no hint of a smile. "After all, today is a day of triumph – a victory for England – and tomorrow we shall celebrate. The Henslowe Players shall be rewarded and I shall personally commission an extended run of *The Spanish Tragedy*."

It took a while for the news to sink in, but then the Henslowe Players started to cheer and whoop in excitement and Trinculo needed no further encouragement to launch into a wincingly awful celebratory jig.

Satisfied, if somewhat perplexed by the reaction of the Henslowe Players, Walsingham moved off to deal with more pressing matters. Tony and Gordon sidled up to Jack and Angus.

"Well, gentlemen, it is good to finally meet you again…"

"Likewise – but I think you might have some explaining to do," Jack replied.

"Of course. But first we need to deal with our next problem."

"What's that?" Jack asked.

But Tony did not have time to respond. The doors at the front of the hall flew open and a royal guard hurried over to Walsingham. He looked terrified.

"The queen! She has been taken! Lady Sarah too…"

Walsingham's face creased up in confusion and shock. "What do you mean?"

The guard stammered, "A man… with pistols, he surprised us, killed the other escorts and took them…" he waved a hand around his head, "into the gardens."

Walsingham unleashed a sort of primeval scream and then lashed out violently with the back of his hand, connecting with the face of the wretched guard. The blow was so ferocious that his nose exploded in a mess of blood.

"Idiots!" Walsingham started to bark orders. "Secure the gates, secure the water gallery, search the gardens and deer park..." He swivelled round to Tony and Gordon. "You – help them!"

Tony turned to Jack and Angus. "As I was about to say, we need to deal with our next problem..."

But Jack had already understood. "Pendelshape's here too."

Into the
Wilderness

Jack, Angus, Tony and Gordon raced down the steps into the gardens. It was getting dark – a crimson sun was setting in a clear winter sky above the oaks of the deer park. The place was crawling with guards – many held flaming torches above their heads.

They paused for breath at the bottom of the stairs, as Tony surveyed the great gardens.

"Pendelshape has managed to kidnap the queen and Lady Sarah?" Jack asked.

"It must be him... desperate to make sure the plot didn't fail," Tony replied.

"Why not just kill her immediately?" Angus said.

"He must have some other warped plan," Gordon said. "And there's something else." He put his hand inside his jacket and took out his time phone. He snapped it open and the telltale yellow light blinked back at them. "We're getting a time signal."

"We've only got minutes to find him..." Tony looked out at the broad vista of the gardens and the deer park beyond and added in frustration, "He could have gone anywhere. Dammit! Where is he?"

Just as the words left Tony's mouth an image popped into Jack's head. It was something from the book that Miss Beattie had shown him. He couldn't have looked at the page for more than five seconds as he leafed through it, but miraculously it now re-appeared in his memory, perfectly formed.

"Maybe he's hiding somewhere, preparing to time travel... where would be a good place to hide?" Gordon said.

Jack knew the answer. "On the outskirts of the palace there is a sort of forest – I'm sure of it."

The others turned towards him. He repeated it. "I think they call it the wilderness – it's a woodland with paths, hedges and thickets. I remember it from Miss Beattie's book. It's the perfect hiding place, and it's just on the edge of the palace grounds. If we move quickly, we might catch them before they go too far."

The light from the sky was fading fast as they sprinted away from the palace. Soon they were working their way along a narrow pathway to the threshold of the wilderness, the huge trees looming over them. The quicker members of the group, including Tony and Gordon, had raced ahead, leaving Jack and Angus slightly behind. As the two boys reached the edge of the forest, they couldn't quite see which way the others had gone.

"Which way?"

"No idea."

"That way then..." Angus chose one of the pathways.

Occasionally they could hear shouts or orders in the distance as the guards kept up a desperate search in the fading light. Jack and Angus pressed on, taking random choices at a further two junctions. Five minutes later and they were utterly lost.

"Stop for a minute," Jack said. "Shall we try and go back?"

"Could do. It's creepy in here."

Suddenly, they heard a loud scream. It was close.

"What was that?"

"I don't know, but I'm not hanging around to find out."

Jack felt himself starting to panic. They ran on, weaving their way through the trees, and then suddenly they found themselves in an oval-shaped clearing, surrounded by thickets and high hedges.

Jack stopped dead in his tracks. The queen and Lady Sarah stood directly ahead of them with their backs pressed up against a huge oak tree on the far side of the clearing. A man stood in front of them, his pistol levelled at the two women. There was sufficient light from the torches for Jack to recognise Pendelshape instantly. He was pointing the gun at the queen and then moved it slowly towards Lady Sarah.

He seemed to be hesitating, confused by the likeness of the two women.

The arrival of Jack and Angus took him by surprise. He swivelled around and, in panic, fired. He missed. Lady Sarah screamed. Jack and Angus dived for cover behind a thicket on the edge of the clearing.

Pendelshape shouted out at them, "You have interfered for the last time."

He fired again but Jack and Angus were well hidden in the thick foliage. Beside himself with frustration, Pendelshape let loose a further two shots, but again they went wide. Swinging the gun back towards Lady Sarah and the queen, he fired again. This time he could not miss. As Jack peered out from the foliage, he saw Lady Sarah's legs give way and she collapsed in a heap. Something inside Jack snapped. He felt a visceral anger well up inside him. He pounced forward, but as he did so, Pendelshape pressed his gun to Elizabeth's head. She stared back, head high, jaw clenched, eyes defiant. Pendelshape pulled the trigger. Nothing. The magazine was empty. Pendelshape screamed in frustration and fumbled for a fresh magazine, but he was too slow. Jack, enraged by the brutal murder of Lady Sarah, leapt up and crashed into Pendelshape's ribcage at full tilt, lifting him clear from the ground and propelling them both forward a full two metres before crunching back to earth. Pendelshape's gun flew free.

Angus, now also up on his feet, looked on with a mixture of dumbfounded astonishment and admiration. Jack was really no match for the stocky and powerful Pendelshape. The teacher had been caught by surprise but he was quick to recover. Enraged, he lashed out with a clenched fist, which caught Jack square on the side of the head. Jack spun sideways, and the world went dark.

"Time you learned... meddling idiot!" Pendelshape growled. He started to crawl around on the ground, cursing angrily and desperately searching for his weapon.

Suddenly, there were voices. Angus shouted, "Help! Over here, we're in the clearing."

A second later, Tony, Gordon and several other royal guardsmen tumbled into sight.

"Over there!" Angus pointed at Pendelshape who was still

scrambling around desperately trying to find his gun.

Tony called out to him, "It's over Pendelshape."

Pendelshape screamed back, "That's what you think... VIGIL is about to be crushed."

"Stand still – or we'll shoot," Gordon shouted.

But Pendelshape was having none of it. He stood up, put his head down, dropped his shoulder and charged directly into the perimeter hedge. Instantly, Tony and Gordon let loose a volley of shots. For a second all was quiet. Suddenly, there was a flash of incandescent white light and for a moment the sky above them was as bright as day. Tony and Gordon rushed over to the hedge through which Pendelshape had escaped.

Tony cursed under his breath. "He's gone. Time signal... this means trouble... we need to get to the safehouse." He turned back to the guards. "You men – take the queen and Lady Sarah back to the palace immediately. We will go ahead and track down the intruder. When you get back to the palace, get Walsingham to send help and search the surrounding area. Now go!"

Tony peered down at Jack. "Are you okay?"

Jack was starting to come round. His head was spinning; he felt like he'd been hit by a bus.

"Hurts like hell... what happened?"

"You just saved the queen's life."

Jack just about had the wherewithal to reply, "But not Lady Sarah's?"

Tony grimaced. "Don't know – she's in a bad way..."

"We've got to go..." Gordon said urgently. "We don't know what Pendelshape is going to do. We need to act while this time signal lasts. We've got a couple of hours at most... come on!"

The guardsmen were already escorting the queen away from the clearing. But as they prepared to leave, she walked over to where they stood. Her voice trembled with emotion.

"Sir, you have saved my life. I must now return to the palace for protection until the area is secured. Report to us tomorrow and you shall be rewarded."

"Your Majesty – we must give chase... the intruder," Tony pressed.

"Yes – you must go." Then, quite spontaneously, she slipped a ring from her finger and pressed it firmly into Jack's hand. "Take this as a token of our thanks. Now Godspeed..." She paused before adding grimly, "And when you find the assassin – kill him – and bring me his head."

Day of Deliverance

It took them fifteen minutes to reach what Tony called the 'safehouse' – a hunting lodge that they had already commandeered in the middle of the deer park about a couple of kilometres from the palace. Jack's head was still throbbing from Pendelshape's punch – and in the dark he had to be supported by Angus and Gordon as Tony led the way through the woodland at a lung-bursting pace. When they entered the lodge, Jack and Angus were surprised to find a third member of VIGIL waiting for them – Theo Joplin.

"We've got a problem," Tony said.

"I noticed: the time signal," Joplin replied.

"Yes, it all went according to plan, except for one thing – Pendelshape has escaped. He could be anywhere."

Angus was not listening. Instead, he was looking at an array of bags and equipment that were stacked up against one wall of the room. "What is all that stuff?"

"Weaponry of various sorts. Provisions. When Joplin came back to reinforce us, VIGIL supplied what we needed to defeat Pendelshape. Don't worry about it just now," Tony said.

Jack's head was spinning. "I need to sit down."

"Sorry, Jack – sit there." Tony pulled out a chair. "Gordon – get the lad an ice pack and break out some of the emergency provisions. We'll all need our blood sugar up. We haven't got much time but let's get ourselves properly organised. What we do next… well, it's life or death now."

Soon they were all sitting round the table inside the main room of the lodge. Joplin had warmed up some tomato soup and they were working their way through bread, cheese and chocolate bars. Jack held the ice pack to his head. Despite the throbbing he was listening intently as the VIGIL team quickly pieced together the events of the last few days to work out their next move.

"So the Taurus transfer went wrong?" Angus said.

"It dumped us in some godforsaken bog north of London. At that point we had no idea where you two were – you could have been dead for all we knew," Tony replied. "We had to lie low and wait for the next signal. To begin with, we froze our butts off in some shack, but then we reckoned we should head to London, because if you or the Revisionists were going to be anywhere it had to be there."

Gordon added, "And finally, we got a time signal. VIGIL located the time phones and identified where you were and where we were – and they told us where we could find you. They also sent Joplin back to help us. Luckily, going to London was the right move – it hasn't taken us long to find you..."

"The torture chamber in that big house?"

"Yes. But we got there too late. We must have arrived after Pendelshape took you away. The letter from Marlowe was our first piece of luck. Pendelshape made a mistake. In his rush to take all those time phones and take you prisoner, he just left it there, lying on a table."

Jack nodded. "You're right, now I think about it, I remember him saying he'd lost it... but I don't think he knew he'd left it behind."

"What did it actually say?" Angus asked.

"Well, now you know," Joplin replied. "It explained the Spanish plot in detail. One of the plotters, Christo, who was already a member of the Henslowe Players, would use the cover of the players' visit to Hampton Court to assassinate the queen. The rest of the letter had details of how various other plotters would encourage sympathetic Catholic aristocrats around the country to rise up on news of the queen's death and provoke a civil war."

Tony continued, "We disguised ourselves as loyalists who had stumbled across the plot and immediately went to Walsingham."

"Ironic – that was just what Marlowe had asked us to do with Fanshawe," Jack said.

"Walsingham already knew that something was afoot – he was

suspicious of Marlowe, who had written the letter and was torn as to whether or not he should send it. Then you turned up. The letter was the last piece of the puzzle. Walsingham moved quickly and decided to set a trap for the plotters at Hampton Court on the opening day of the play."

"The plan worked well," Tony said. "Although, Angus, what you did was a surprise. Gordon was about to take out Christo, but you were just too quick."

"So... who was that other queen – you know, Lady Sarah?" Jack paused, his voice quiet. "Will she die?"

"I don't know. I'm afraid it is likely. She was incredibly brave to act as the queen's double," Tony replied. "She looks quite like the queen... and dressed up in all that garb and in character presiding over the play, how on earth was Christo to know any different? It's not as if he'd ever seen a photo of the queen. In the wilderness it also confused Pendelshape – probably bought us some time."

"And the crossbow men?"

"Royal guards, disguised as courtiers. The entire thing was a set up – the whole audience – the queen's double, everything. We hadn't much time, but it came together on the night."

"You knew that Whitsun and Gift would be there?"

"We were pretty sure, and we hoped Pendelshape would be there as well, together with any other Revisionists, so we could get them all at the same time. The Revisionist plan was to piggyback on the existing Spanish plot. They want their interventions to be as 'light touch' as possible – saves them work and makes it all cleaner."

"You and the crossbow men were ready," Angus said. "Brilliant."

"Losing Pendelshape was not so brilliant, though. Unless we can nail him, we're done for."

Joplin looked at Jack, concentrating hard. "Jack, after Pendelshape took you prisoner, was there anything, anything at all, that he said about his plans to change history?"

"It was pretty amazing. He showed us a kind of game where Spain conquers England and then all of the Americas and that becomes a basis for some sort of global domination. He said there was a way of measuring how it would be better than our present history – real history, if you like. Called it 'UI' or something."

"Utility Index?" Joplin looked at his colleagues with ashen-faced incredulity. "They must have developed the causal modelling to a very sophisticated degree. That is very worrying."

"Er, sorry?" Angus said.

Joplin explained. "If this software can really model intended changes into the future with such precision, that is a truly powerful ability. It is a capability that we in VIGIL certainly never thought possible. Basically, they can play God."

"Sometimes I reckon Pendelshape thinks he *is* God," Jack said.

Joplin rubbed the back of his neck. "This is very serious, Jack. Did Pendelshape say anything else – was he more *specific*?"

Jack thought for a moment about what Pendelshape had told them. "He said ideally he needed to do two things. First, he said Elizabeth must die to create disorder across the country – a sort of power vacuum. Then he said the Spanish Armada needed to succeed. The Spanish troops under the Duke of Parma in the Netherlands could then just walk in and take control. In fact, he seemed to think even if they didn't manage to kill the queen, the second part of the plan could still work, as long as the Armada succeeded."

"The Armada – did he say anything more about that?"

Angus piped up, "He mentioned a battle... Grave – something."

Joplin banged the table. "Gravelines! I knew it. That confirms it." Joplin jumped to his feet and started to pace the room. "I have been piecing together a theory based on the information your father gave us and our knowledge of history. Gravelines was a sea battle that took place in the east of the English Channel. The defeat of the Armada was down to many things... but if there was one point where you wanted to make a decisive change in favour of the Spanish fleet, Gravelines would be it. Gravelines was the point where the English ships engaged and damaged the great ships of the Armada. After Gravelines, the Armada fled up the English coast, badly battered but still intact. After that point though, the storms got them. Those that did survive the wrecks and struggled ashore were often murdered and robbed. If you wanted to change the outcome of events for Phillip II and Spain and allow a Spanish victory, the history of England, Spain and the world would be dramatically different. It would be Spain's day of deliverance."

"How would you do it, though? I mean, how can Pendelshape take on all those English ships on his own?" Jack asked.

Joplin shook his head. "I don't know. But you're right Jack, you would need some way to destroy the English fleet. Quickly and easily. Some form of military superiority. With the fleet at the bottom of the Channel, London and England would be open for the Armada to transport the Duke of Parma's Spanish troops from the Netherlands into England, just as they planned. England had no army that could resist them. It would only be a matter of weeks before all of England was in Phillip II's hands. Your information confirms my theory: Gravelines is the critical event. I am convinced the Revisionists will use this time signal to stage an intervention. Pendelshape will want to get on with it." Joplin gestured at the bags of equipment arranged along one wall of the room. "We need to get going – let's take what we need from that lot and Tony, you need to code the time phones for the battle of Gravelines – 8th August 1588."

"Okay." Tony opened a thin briefcase on the table and took out two time phones. He handed one to Jack and one to Angus. "Yours – and don't lose them this time."

Jack picked up the time phone. "Hold on, you're not expecting us to come as well?"

"Of course. It's like Inchquin said – you two are fully paid-up members of VIGIL now – part of the team, and where we're going, we'll need all the help we can get."

"What – you're taking us into a war zone?"

"No mistake, Jack – this is war."

Gravelines
Graveyard

Jack and Angus were squashed into a wooden barrel that was open at the top. Above them was clear sky. Jack popped his head over the edge of the barrel and immediately wished he hadn't. They were suspended forty metres in the air above a choppy, grey sea. Seconds ago, before the time transport, they had been in the safehouse. The barrel swung from side to side in a giddy arc. It felt like some sort of mad fairground attraction. In fact, they were in the crow's nest of an English battleship. But this was no ordinary battleship – they were soaring high above the deck of *The Revenge*, Sir Francis Drake's flagship, as it led the English line towards the Spanish Armada. The ship's motion in the water was transmitted through the masts so that at the crow's nest the movement was wildly accentuated. Jack's response was to cling on to the edge of the barrel to avoid being flung into the abyss below. But his terror was replaced by goggle-eyed incredulity when he surveyed the scene beneath them.

The sea around them was thick with ships of all shapes and sizes – massive galleons, barges and hulks – some powered by sail, some by oars and some by both. Everywhere, they could see white canvas sails billowing in a freshening wind and a forest of masts, fighting tops and the complex tracery of rigging. The sails of the great Spanish galleons were emblazoned with giant red crosses. Behind them, the English ships were adorned with the St George cross, the royal standard and the rose of the House of Tudor.

"Ships... everywhere..." Angus gasped in amazement.

"Look..."

Jack pointed to a very large Spanish galleon on which *The Revenge*

A scene from the battle of Gravelines

was rapidly closing in. They could even make out the lettering on its side – *San Martin* – the Spanish flagship. With its raised castles, fore and aft, it towered over *The Revenge*, which by contrast was built for speed and agility. They were close enough to see men with muskets and arquebuses in the fighting tops of the *San Martin* and lines of close-packed soldiers along the rail of the decks ready to fire. Jack knew that the Spanish would try to grapple and board the English ship, but they had already learned from bitter, earlier experiences on the Armada campaign that the English would not allow them to do so. Instead, using their greater manoeuvrability, the English would keep just out of grappling distance and one by one they would use their superior gunnery to pick off and pulverise each lumbering Spanish galleon, like a pack of hungry wolves descending on a helpless, tethered cow.

"Cling on. Looks like we're going in," Angus said.

The Revenge was less than twenty metres from the *San Martin* when first her bow guns and then her broadside guns erupted in cannon fire. Although Jack and Angus were above the main action, they were still in danger, but the spectacle had a hypnotic momentum and they stared in wonder as they inched past the *San Martin*. Jack could see that there were holes in her sails already and some of her magnificent carpentry had been reduced to matchwood. They could hear screaming from the close-packed decks and upper works as chain-shot, hail-shot and cube-shot, each designed to maim, kill and destroy in its own unique and bloody way, took their terrible toll.

Jack looked away and tried to focus on his feet and the inside of the barrel, but Angus continued to stare – his face lined in horror.

"Those poor guys..."

Finally, *The Revenge* drifted clear, but the plight of the *San Martin* was not over. Behind them, the rest of Drake's squadron, followed by Frobisher's squadron, headed by *The Triumph* and Hawkins's squadron in *The Victory*, lined up in turn to pummel the *San Martin*. They now saw other ships of the Armada rallying to protect the *San Martin*, but the English cannons pounded relentlessly in a progressive rumble as the cannons fired successively along the length of each ship.

Suddenly, a round of chain shot from a Spanish ship spun through the upper rigging of *The Revenge*. It hit the upper mast and sliced through the rope that tethered the crow's nest. Jack and Angus felt the barrel lurch violently as the securing ropes fell away. The barrel inverted itself, although somehow it remained hanging by a single thread. Jack and Angus could do nothing to save themselves. Sliding out of the upturned barrel, Angus was propelled through empty space, but before he could reach any speed, he slammed into a cross-spar that broke his fall. He clawed desperately at a flapping rope secured from the mast above, which he finally managed to reach and cling on to. But then, a second shot shredded the cross-spar, which promptly collapsed, leaving Angus suspended in the rigging, twenty metres up, swinging from side to side like a human pendulum.

Jack was only slightly luckier. As he was launched deckwards, the furious assault from the Spanish ship dislodged the upper gallant and its huge billowing sail floated seawards like a giant parachute. Jack, accelerating rapidly through the air, landed square on top of the rolling canvas as it floated down. The sail deposited him gracefully on the foredeck of *The Revenge*, before folding in on itself and floating gently into the sea. Jack had no time to reflect on his incredible escape. The deck of *The Revenge* was alive with men fighting for their lives. He craned his neck upwards, searching the rigging for any sign of Angus, but he could see nothing.

"You there!" a man shouted. "Gun deck!"

With no time to think, Jack found himself being bundled below. The gun deck was a single, low-ceilinged cavern. The massive trunks of the ship's masts passed directly through it, rising from the floor and up through the roof. Inside the gun deck, Jack could see that every timber was black with spent powder. There were huge iron guns decorated with coats of arms, which rested on massive carriages held on wheels cut from whole sections of tree trunk. The oak planking around them was grooved where the guns had been run in and out time and again. Piles of shot and cartridges of black powder were stacked in the lockers by the guns alongside ramrods, powder scoops and match cord. Suddenly, a cannon ball from a Spanish ship ripped though the planking of the gun deck, unleashing a blizzard of splinters. Jack saw one man collapse, impaled by a shard of wood. But his comrades kept grimly to the routine of their work. As the men sweated, the master gunners barked orders. It was a scene from hell, and Jack knew that if he stayed he would die. Nobody noticed as he bolted back up on deck.

But the deck of *The Revenge* was more nightmarish than the scene below. Jack gagged on the smell of gunpowder, which was heavy in the air. The smoke from the guns cloaked the water in great billows of dark mist causing ships to appear and disappear like hulking beasts. The bodies of the injured and dying lay across the deck of *The Revenge*, but it was nothing compared to the damage to the Spanish ships. Some ships were close and Jack could see that their sails were tattered and torn and their splintered decks strewn with the dead, blood pouring from the scuppers as they heeled in the wind.

"Down here!"

Jack swivelled round. "Angus!"

"How did you...?"

"Never mind about that. I found the others – come on!"

Jack followed Angus into the aft-castle of *The Revenge* and down into the captain's cabin. It was strewn with broken furniture, books and the half-emptied bags that Jack had seen at the safe house. Tony was near the shattered rear windows wrestling with some sort of large tubular device. To one side, Joplin knelt by Gordon, who groaned in pain.

"What happened to him?" Jack asked.

"Gun shot – got him in the shoulder," Joplin said. "Keep your heads down – the cabin has already been hit twice."

"Is he going to be okay?"

"Think so – if we can get him home quickly while we still have the time signal." Joplin nodded towards Tony. "But you two need to help over there – we've got a problem."

Then Jack heard it. Over the sound of the cannon, gun fire and sailors' cries, they could hear the shrill whine of an aircraft engine and a loud mechanical whirring. Jack and Angus peered gingerly through the windows at the rear of the captain's cabin. Emerging from the

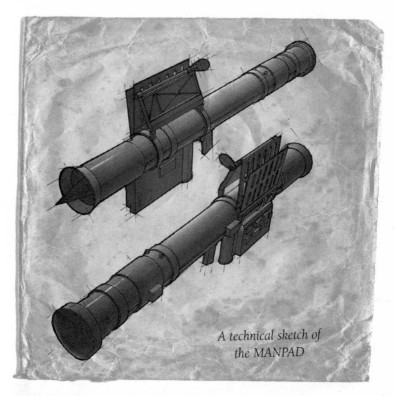

*A technical sketch of
the MANPAD*

billowing clouds of gun smoke, a black military helicopter appeared, hovering a mere ten metres above the water. The machine was utterly incongruous with the great sailing ships of the Armada.

Joplin had said that Pendelshape would require a 'decisive military advantage' to defeat the English fleet and give the Spanish the naval superiority they would need to stage the invasion of England. It was now clear how that advantage would be achieved and how the Armada would snatch victory from the jaws of defeat. In a final throw of the dice, Pendelshape was about to give Philip II his day of deliverance and change the course of history for ever.

"What is *that?*" Jack said.

"Helicopter gun-ship," Tony answered. "Pendelshape and the Revisionists have transported it back on the time signal. We got here at the right time."

"It's a what?"

"A Westland WAH-64 Apache – the British army version. It's got the Rolls-Royce engines, a chain gun that will fire over six hundred rounds a minute, and those pods on the side carry hellfire and CRV7 rockets. It's a beast," Angus said in admiration.

"Never mind that – Pendelshape is inside with a co-pilot and God knows what else. We haven't got much time before he takes out the whole of the English fleet – and us with it."

Jack and Angus looked at the strange device that Tony was wrestling with as he spoke. It was like a fat steel tube. There was a large sight attached to the top and a trigger underneath.

"What is that thing? Looks like a bazooka."

"It's a MANPAD," Tony said.

"Is that a real word?"

"Does it really matter?" Tony replied in frustration. "It's a Man Portable Air Defence System. One of the toys we brought back with us. There..." Tony said triumphantly, "we're ready."

Angus nodded through the window. "Well, I hope so, because we have incoming."

The helicopter pirouetted on its vertical axis, sniffing out its first prey. The English flagship seemed a good place to start and the machine was directly level with the stern of *The Revenge*. Suddenly, the chain gun hanging from its belly exploded into life and bullets ripped into the upper part of the cabin unleashing a blizzard of splinters over the heads of Jack and Angus, who hugged the floor. Tony was not so lucky. One second he was holding the MANPAD by the window, the next he was gone – flung from one side of the cabin to the other by a single round from the helicopter gun. He lay on the floor, clutching his upper arm, cursing bitterly. The firing stopped and the helicopter hung in the air, gathering itself for a final assault. Jack and Angus rushed over to help Tony.

"Don't worry about me," he said through gritted teeth. "Get him before he kills us all."

Angus rushed back, grabbed the launcher and heaved it up onto his shoulder. He staggered towards the window, which had been completely obliterated by the storm of bullets. He aimed at the helicopter, closed his eyes and squeezed the trigger.

Nothing happened.

Jack was now at his side and they could both see the helicopter inching forward for the final kill.

"I think you need to switch it on."

Jack flicked a switch on the side of the launcher and it hummed into life.

This time, Angus kept his eyes open and aimed. He fired and the rocket fizzed from the muzzle of the launcher and smashed into the housing beneath the rotor blades. There was an explosion, but then the smoke cleared and, incredibly, the helicopter was hanging in the air.

In desperation, Jack turned to Tony at the back of the cabin. "He's still there!"

But then the tone of the engine changed and the rhythmic whirring of the blades seemed to falter and slow down. The machine hung for a moment longer and then dropped like a stone into the sea. Jack and Angus looked on as the two pilots struggled to free themselves from the water rising up inside the cockpit. As he looked down from the stern cabin of *The Revenge*, Jack clearly saw Pendelshape raging at them from the cockpit.

Sultan of Spin

Beneath his feet, Jack saw the shimmering eddies of electricity consolidate and then morph into the steel platform of the Taurus. The heavy metal struts that bounded the inner shell of the great machine gradually came into focus and the features of the control room beyond the thick green glass of the blast screen became clearer. The blast screen was lowered and a number of people in the control centre came forward – they were clapping and cheering. Jack blinked. He could see Inchquin, the Rector, Beattie and, right at the front, his mum, Carole, beaming from ear to ear. They were home.

Jack could hear the hum from the generators powering down as he and Angus made their way down the gantry from the Taurus. The medical team rushed forward to help down the injured Tony and Gordon, who were immediately dispatched to the underground surgery. Carole Christie rushed forward to hug Jack and seconds later Inchquin and then the Rector were shaking their hands. It was over.

Following a medical examination and a meal, they decamped to VIGIL's Situation Room to debrief. The team sat round the same table where Inchquin had chaired the first war council, on hearing the news leaked by Jack's father following his bust-up with Pendelshape. They spent the next hour picking through their experiences in the sixteenth century – supported by analysis from the rest of the VIGIL team. Jack struggled to get his head round it all.

"So how do you know that our mission was a success? Is it just because you know we don't have to go back and, kind of, do any more 'tidying up'?"

Inchquin smiled. "I know it is difficult to understand, but it is self-evident. We are all still here and history as we remember it is the same before your mission as it is now – a very short time later."

"But, but – what if Pendelshape had succeeded?" Angus said.

"If the Revisionist mission had been a success we would be living in a very different world. Perhaps we wouldn't exist at all. We don't really know for sure what the consequences would be – and for that reason alone it is extremely dangerous to meddle in history."

"When we met Pendelshape, he said that the Revisionists' modelling techniques were now so sophisticated that they would somehow be able to ring-fence themselves from the changes they made. So they'd, you know, make changes to history so the future was better, but kind of keep themselves and their Taurus separate and in control." Jack looked at Inchquin with a furrowed brow. "Is that *possible*?"

Inchquin shook his head. "It's called 'lineage isolation'. They clearly *think* it's possible – and it may be, perhaps with repeated interventions – but we think it would be utter madness."

Jack's brain was working overtime. "By what you're saying then... does that mean we kind of know that the Revisionists will never be successful, because, you know, if they had – history would already be different?"

Inchquin smiled. "Very good, Jack. Indeed that is one theory – that history as we know it already reflects what has happened, including any interventions that the Revisionists have made, and, in fact, interventions we have made to stop them."

Angus moaned. "Sorry – I'm lost – this is a complete mindbender."

"The point is, Angus, much of this time theory is conjecture. However clever the scientists are, we just don't understand it well enough. We are on the edge of the unknown, but our position is clear: the human race is not some sort of experiment in a petri dish to fiddle around with."

"Well one thing is for sure," Joplin said breezily, "we now know much more about what did happen – including the plot to kill the queen."

"What do you mean, Theo?"

"Well, as you know, the plot already exists in the historical archive;

however, it's practically a footnote. But we know from what we saw at Hampton Court that it was one of the most dramatic of the many plots against Elizabeth in the late sixteenth century. My theory now is that Walsingham suppressed much of the detail, including the death of Lady Sarah."

"Why?"

"Although unearthing the plot and trapping the assassins so brilliantly at Hampton Court was a triumph for England, and a personal triumph for Walsingham, on reflection he clearly decided that the whole thing was too close for comfort – particularly the narrow escape in the wilderness. The queen could have been killed and the kingdom could have been thrown into turmoil. Walsingham must have considered it much better to perpetuate the image of the Faerie Queene – untouchable, inviolate, supreme – rather than publicise the reality of the plot too enthusiastically."

"No decapitated heads were sent to Philip II?"

"Far too unsubtle. And remember Elizabeth's speech in the hall..."

Jack nodded.

"Well, that must have been quietly suppressed too. Later it was re-used, of course. It is now remembered as part of her famous speech at Tilbury, which was delivered more than a year later, actually as the threat of the Armada passed."

"Elizabeth – the first sultan of spin!" Joplin chortled at his own joke. "She'd do some of our own politicians proud."

"What happened to Marlowe?"

"A bit of a mystery. We know that the Spanish took him into hiding following the incident in Cambridge. When the plot fell through, there was no evidence for the Spanish to really pin the blame on him. We think Walsingham continued to use him as a spy, but may have finally lost patience a few years later. Marlowe was murdered – a dagger above the right eye – some say it was a drunken brawl, but others believe it was an assassination, as all three of the other men who were with him when he died worked for Walsingham and his brother."

There was silence for a moment and for some reason the words from Marlowe's portrait ghosted through Jack's mind:

What feeds me destroys me.

"One thing, then..." Angus said, "what about a helicopter appearing in the middle of the Armada? I've never heard of that before – you're not telling me that Walsingham hushed that up too."

Joplin laughed. "Good point. My theory is that there was such confusion during the battle – the smoke, the noise – you saw what it was like – that few eye witnesses recorded the event. Remember, it was only there for a few minutes. Those who did see it, and survived, referred, glassy-eyed, to a 'fiery monster descending into the sea' or 'a lightning bolt from the finger of God' – all explanations that historians readily put down to the religious hysteria of the time or post-traumatic stress disorder suffered by the witnesses. Remember that many of the Spanish died and actually a lot of the English did too – but after the battle; there was no money to pay for their care. Anyway, the reports that existed were felt to be nonsense and were, rightly, treated as such later on by serious historians."

"But we know better," the Rector said as he stood up and pointed to an electronic map on the wall. "We have already dispatched a salvage crew to the English Channel to determine if anything was left of the helicopter wreck at the bottom of the sea, even though four hundred years have passed since it sank. If we can identify bones or teeth in the wreck, it will prove that Pendelshape and whoever else was in that blasted contraption are gone for good – and with them, hopefully the entire Revisionist cause."

By the time Jack and Angus climbed wearily into Carole Christie's battered old VW Golf, it was nearly midnight.

"I rang your parents, Angus, to say you would be late and would sleep over with us tonight," Carole said.

"Thanks, Carole." Angus slapped his forehead. "Hey! I nearly forgot."

"What?" Jack said.

"It's the rugby final tomorrow."

Jack grinned. "You're going to walk it after what we've been through."

Taser Town

It was a beautiful spring day. Jack cycled his mountain bike up the old driveway at Cairnfield and then onto the main road that led up the long hill into Soonhope High Street. It was a busy Saturday lunchtime and the world and his wife seemed to be out. Angus was waiting outside Gino's with a big grin on his face. He saw Jack and waved something in the air. It was the rugby trophy.

"We won!"

"Good stuff – did you score?"

"Just one try." Angus jerked his head towards the café. "Come on – chip butties to celebrate – then I've got to head home."

Gino was delighted to see them. In fact he was so delighted, that he immediately closed the shop and turfed everyone else out, making some excuse about a gas leak.

"You've had a big adventure, eh?" he winked at them conspiratorially. "You are both big VIGIL heroes. What can I get you? It's on the house." He grinned. "Don't tell me: double Gino-chino, extra shot, full fat, with caramel and extra cream..." Then Angus and Gino announced in unison, "And don't forget the cherry." Gino thought this was absolutely hilarious and his belly wobbled as he laughed uproariously.

"Chip butties too please, Gino."

Jack and Angus settled into one of the booths and straight away Angus started fiddling with the large plastic tomato-shaped ketchup holder. He squeezed it so the sauce just oozed out of the top, before releasing his grip so that it was sucked back in again with a satisfying squelch.

"That's disgusting," Jack said after Angus had squidged the bottle for the third time.

"Sorry," Angus replied. "Hey, have you still got it? You know, the ring or whatever it was old queenie gave you?"

Jack smiled and reached into his pocket. He placed the ring on the table. It glinted up at them.

Angus looked agog. "It's a whopper. What's that green thing?"

"Emerald – stupid. That's the stone. The ring is gold."

"What do you think it's worth?"

Jack shrugged. "Thousands, maybe tens of thousands..."

"*Awesome*. You going to keep it?"

"Of course. It's mine. Queen Elizabeth I of England gave it to me – the Faerie Queene. I saved her life, her kingdom and the human race... though, granted, you did help," Jack said, smiling.

Angus just laughed.

"Hey, I brought something else to show you," Jack said. "Really weird this... I mean almost as weird as some of the stuff we saw."

Jack pulled from his bag the large history book that Miss Beattie had loaned him.

"Remember Beattie gave this to me before we went back? It's got all sorts of pictures and stuff about Queen Elizabeth and the sixteenth century..." Jack thumbed through the pages. "Check that out."

Jack pointed at the small colour frame at the bottom of one of the pages. It was one he had noticed when he'd first leafed through the book, entitled 'Elizabethan Troupe'. It was a simple colour plate of a group of actors in various costumes. There was one dressed as a court jester and next to him, in stark contrast, another dressed as a monk. There was a third who looked slightly more important – like a country gentleman with a fine cloak and a neat, pointed beard.

"No way!" Angus nearly slid off his seat. "It's the Marlowe players at Corpus Christi and that's got to be Fanshawe, Trinculo and Monk..."

"And?" Jack said knowingly.

Eyeing the picture more closely, Angus spotted two further figures off to one side. One was tall and broad with longish black hair. The other was shorter, more slender, and had a shock of blond hair. For a moment Angus could not place them – then he realised – it was the two of them: Angus and Jack.

"Didn't really notice it before. But that's not all. There's a picture of the battle of Gravelines – you know, showing the 'fiery god'."

Angus was not impressed, "Doesn't look much like a helicopter to me. Certainly not a WAH-64 Apache armed with a chain gun and CRV7 rockets."

"Well, as Joplin said, that's the problem with eyewitness accounts."

"And historians – they're clearly all rubbish."

The shop was quiet for a moment. Gino broke the silence, humming behind the counter as he prepared the chip butties.

"I nearly forgot!" Jack said, pulling out his mobile. "Got a message..."

"Oh yeah? Who's it from?"

"Dad." Jack scrolled down the emails and waved the device in Angus's face. "Look."

Angus squinted at the text and read aloud:

```
"Let us go in together;
And still your fingers on your lips, I pray.
The time is out of joint; O cursed spite,
That ever I was born to set it right!"
```

"It's that weird quote again – about the world being broken and someone having to sort it out. Wasn't that what you said?"

Jack smiled. "Sort of – the verse from *Hamlet*."

Angus read on.

```
Jack,
Sources tell me that you have had quite an
adventure. You and Angus are very brave,
young men. I have heard about Pendelshape's
attempt to change history - it was poorly
planned and badly executed. It is not how
I would have done it, were I still in charge.
Most importantly, you must know that I would
```

never have put you in such danger.

I see now that you are finding your own way in life, and I understand that it may not be the way that I have chosen. You have to make your own choices, Jack. Despite this, I still hope that we might meet one day, talk as friends and perhaps even find a way to make peace with VIGIL.

But what I really wanted to say is this: I am proud of you.

Dad

Angus looked up. "Wow. What do you think he will do next?"

Jack shrugged. "No idea. He's in a pretty desperate situation… a fugitive. Must be tough – on the run from VIGIL."

Jack quickly pocketed the mobile as Gino brought over the Gino-chinos and the chip butties, taking his own place next to them at the booth, with a small espresso in front of him.

"You did very well, lads. The whole team is proud."

Francesca, Gino's daughter, emerged from the back of the café. She was burdened with large bags of shopping. Gino winced, and whispered to Jack and Angus, "Watch it boys – she's in a bad mood."

Sure enough Francesca marched up the aisle between the booths and dumped the shopping at Gino's feet.

"Why am I the only one who does any work around here?" she demanded.

"Hi Francesca," Angus said breezily. Francesca returned his greeting with a withering stare.

"I'm sick of this pokey little shop and I'm sick of this pokey little town…"

Gino looked hurt, "My dear…"

But the girl had clearly had enough. "There's nothing to do here…

nothing ever happens..."

Gino's moody daughter could not have been more wrong. Around the booth next to them, there was a disturbance in the air, then a blinding flash of white light. In front of them appeared a tall man with a rich tan and chiselled features. He wore a fine black cloak. Next to him were two shorter, powerfully built men. One had a badly disfigured eye and a scar that stretched from his forehead, across the side of his eye and down his cheek. The last time Jack and Angus had seen Delgado, Hegel and Plato was in a torture chamber underneath a house on the outskirts of Elizabethan London. It was just before Jack had tricked them with the time phone and zapped them into hyperspace. Little did he know that they would be transported to Gino Turinelli's Italian café in the middle of Soonhope High Street.

Although they looked dazed and confused, it did not take long for Delgado to gather his wits. He had no idea where he was, but he recognised Jack and Angus and he drew his sword. Francesca screamed. Gino was the first to react. He leaped from the booth and dived over the counter of the café. For a portly man he moved surprisingly quickly. In an instant Plato was after him, sword in hand. He jumped up onto the counter and swung his sword around his head, dislodging great lumps of plaster from the ceiling and sending plates, glasses, bottles and jars flying around the café. Gino slowly got to his feet and raised his hands from behind the counter in a gesture of surrender. Plato stopped waving his sword around and from his position on the counter, lowered it menacingly so it touched the base of Gino's throat. He looked back over his shoulder to Delgado and awaited his orders. Hegel grabbed Francesca from behind and held a dagger to her cheek. Francesca whimpered. Delgado approached Jack and Angus with his sword outstretched and they cowered back in the booth.

Jack glanced over at Gino who was trembling and had his eyes closed. But Jack noticed that in one of his outstretched hands he was grasping something... a mobile phone.

Delgado hissed at Jack, "Where are we – what kind of *witchcraft* is this?" He no longer spoke in the calm and collected way he had done in the cellar. He was confused and scared. This made him dangerous and unpredictable – he might do anything.

"You speak, my friend," he glanced over at Hegel, who pressed the flat side of his knife to Francesca's cheek, "or the girl dies."

Suddenly, in the distance, they could hear the sound of a police siren. Jack's heart leaped – somehow Gino had made the emergency call.

Delgado heard the noise too and he became more agitated. "What is this noise?"

He left Jack and Angus unguarded for a moment, crept gingerly forward to the plate-glass window at the front of the café and peered into the street beyond. The good people of Soonhope, oblivious to the strange events taking place inside the town's favourite Italian café, were going about their business – as on any other Saturday lunchtime. Jack could see the look on Delgado's face as he gazed from one end of the High Street to the other. It was the same expression of stupid shock that Jack must have shown when he regained consciousness on top of the tower at Fotheringhay Castle. In a way, what Delgado saw was normal. There were people out there, walking, talking and going about their business. The large building at one end of the street looked oddly familiar – a church built not long after. But the people were dressed in an extraordinary way. There were no horses or carts. And why was the street strewn with large, coloured boxes... on wheels?

Delgado was still standing paralysed in front of the window when three distinctive metal boxes drew up outside – ones with flashing lights on the top. The people of Soonhope had no time to register that the most exciting event in their High Street's history was happening right before their eyes. The plate-glass window of Gino's café shattered and before Delgado could react, the two dart-electrodes from the taser gun hit him square in the chest. He screamed as the electric charge coursed through his body. Behind him, Hegel and Plato experienced the same fate, as police stormed in from the back of the café. Incapacitated, the three men were quickly bundled into the back of a police van and driven off at speed. Naturally, VIGIL's reach also extended to the local police force. The café was quickly cordoned off.

Day of Deliverance

Soon afterwards, Tony arrived; his shoulder was still heavily strapped from his injury. He looked around the café. Glass from the smashed front window had sprayed across the floor and broken crockery was strewn everywhere. Policemen were inspecting the debris. In one corner, Gino tried to comfort Francesca, who sobbed in his arms. Jack and Angus had not budged from their position in the booth.

"I don't know what it is with you two," Tony said, "but you always make such a lot of mess."

The Last Act

Jack knew what he had to do. Clutching his chest to stem the bleeding, he staggered across to where his uncle sat cowering behind the long banqueting table. The food and drink was still laid out, untouched. Jack mounted the table and fixed his eyes menacingly on his uncle, who sank back into his chair, shaking. There was to be no mercy and Jack did not hesitate – he thrust the sword into his uncle's heart.

The first performance of *Hamlet* at Soonhope High was over. The audience of parents and local worthies gave the tired but happy cast a well-deserved standing ovation. As rehearsed, Jack held out his hand to the wings and Miss Beattie came onto the stage, blushing slightly. She gave a little bow and received a bunch of flowers from one of the cast. There were calls of "Bravo!" from the audience. After a few more bows, the curtains closed.

Jack and Angus joined the backstage party to celebrate the success of the opening night.

"We'll make an actor of you yet, Angus," Jack said.

"Think it was watching the Henslowe Players for all those hours."

"Nice of Beattie to give you a chance..." Jack looked round the room. "Here she is now – looks pleased."

"And here come the Rector and Inchquin..."

"They're out in force tonight."

"And your mum."

In a minute Jack and Angus were surrounded by the Rector, Inchquin and Beattie.

"Congratulations!" The Rector put out his hand. "A fine performance... you've done the school proud."

"We've had a bit of a crash course over the last week," Jack replied.

Inchquin smiled, "So I hear, Jack, so I hear." He lowered his voice, to ensure that they were not overheard, "Which brings me onto another matter. You should know. Our salvage team finally found the wreck of Pendelshape's helicopter in the English Channel."

"Oh?"

"Yes. Apparently it was all silted up and badly corroded. It's been lying there for four hundred years, after all."

"What about the bodies – any, er, remains of the people inside... Pendelshape?" Jack asked.

There was a flash of concern on the Rector's face. "No, Jack. We found nobody – nobody at all."

The Taurus and Time Travel – Some Notes

The Taurus and its energy source always stay in one place. In order to move through time and space, the traveller needs to have physical contact with a time phone, which is controlled and tracked through a set of codes connected with the Taurus. Time travel is only possible, however, when the Taurus has enough energy and when there is a strong carrier signal. As Jack and Angus have discovered, the signal can be as unpredictable as the weather. The time signals are also highly variable – periods of time open up and then close, like shifting sands, so that no location is constantly accessible. Deep time is a specific constraint, which means that the traveller cannot visit a time period less than thirty years in the past. Anything more recent is a no-go zone. Finally, there is the 'Armageddon Scenario', which suggests that, if you revisit the same point of space–time more than once, you dramatically increase the risk of a continuum meltdown. Imagine space-time as a piece of tissue paper – each visit makes a hole in that tissue paper, as if you had pushed through the tissue with your finger. The tissue would hold together for a while, but with too many holes, it would disintegrate. It is dangerous, therefore, to repeat trips to the same point. The precise parameters of this constraint are not known and have not, of course, been tested.

A chart of the Armada's course from Calais and around the coast of Scotland and Ireland, 1588.

Day of Deliverance

BACKGROUND INFORMATION

In *Day of Deliverance*, Jack and Angus travel back in time to one of the most extraordinary periods of history – Elizabethan England. This was a time when Spain was England's greatest rival, when a glamorous queen called Elizabeth ruled the nation, and when colourful characters such as Francis Drake, Walter Raleigh and Mary, Queen of Scots made their mark on history. The notes below give a little more information on the places that Jack and Angus go and the people they encounter on their adventure.

Who was Elizabeth I? (p.22)

Elizabeth I was born in 1533 and died in 1603, ruling as the Queen of England and Ireland from 1558 until her death. Elizabeth was the daughter of Henry VIII and Anne Boleyn, and was the last monarch of the Tudor dynasty. Elizabeth became queen in turbulent times – when England was racked by religious turmoil, and threatened by civil war and invasion. Despite this, Elizabeth had a clear agenda, and one of her first campaigns as queen was to establish an English Protestant church, which has evolved into what we know today as the Church of England.

Although she was a queen with many admirers and courtiers, Elizabeth never married, despite pressure from advisers. She was headstrong and proud, and would not let her heart rule her head. In government, Elizabeth was more moderate than her father, and was not always vocal in foreign affairs. The defeat of the Spanish Armada, however, connected her with one of the greatest victories in world military history.

Day of Deliverance

What was the Renaissance? (p.21)

The Renaissance was a cultural revolution that spread from Italy in the fourteenth and fifteenth centuries. This period of change began with a rediscovery of Greek and Roman ideas, and from it some of the world's finest art and architecture was conceived. The influence was slow to spread to England, partly due to the effect of the Wars of the Roses – a series of civil wars fought between the rival houses of Lancaster and York for the throne of England. All this began to change when Elizabeth was at the height of her power in the late sixteenth century.

During Elizabeth's reign, a number of gifted Dutch painters sought asylum from Spanish persecution and were supported by the queen who was herself enthusiastic about education, poetry, plays and theatre. In architecture, new 'Prodigy' houses were built – beautiful buildings like Hardwick Hall, Montacute, Longleat, Wollaton Hall and Burghley House. In literature, there was an explosion of creative energy – John Donne and Sir Philip Sidney in poetry, and Marlowe, Kyd and Jonson in theatre. In the years to come, of course, Shakespeare would become the most celebrated playwright, and the man who changed the face of the English language forever.

Song and dance also developed during Elizabeth's reign. Like her father, Henry VIII, Elizabeth was a talented musician. A favourite dance of the queen's was the *volta*, in which the man lifted his partner high in the air.

What was the speech at Tilbury? (p.180)

Elizabeth's speech in *Day of Deliverance* is delivered at Hampton Court. This scene, of course, is fictitious, but the words are real. It was first thought that Elizabeth gave this speech as the Armada fleet approached, but historians now believe that it was carefully refined after the attack and published widely.

Did Mary, Queen of Scots really have her head cut off? If so, why? (p.58)

Mary, Queen of Scots was born in 1542 and was executed at Fotheringhay Castle on 8th February 1587. Mary was the cousin of

Elizabeth I, and reigned as Queen of Scotland from 1542 to 1567. Unlike Elizabeth, Mary had many husbands in her lifetime – in 1558, she married Francis, Dauphin of France, and following his death she married her first cousin, Lord Darnley. When Darnley also died, she married James Hepburn, the Earl of Bothwell, who was generally believed to be Darnley's murderer. During an uprising, Mary abdicated the throne in favour of her son, James VI, and fled to England seeking the protection of her cousin, Elizabeth.

Elizabeth, however, did not open her arms to her cousin. Mary was widely thought to be the legitimate sovereign of England, and, therefore, a great threat to Elizabeth's throne. In the end, Walsingham implicated Mary in the Babington Plot and she was finally tried and executed for treason.

Does Hampton Court still exist today? (p.148)

Yes – Hampton Court Palace is one of the most famous buildings in the UK and is situated on the river near Kingston upon Thames. The palace was the centre of court and political life during the sixteenth and seventeenth centuries, and was built to host monarchs, their courtiers and hundreds of servants. It has over a thousand rooms and is set within stunning gardens and parkland.

Did people really drink beer instead of water in Elizabethan England? (p.99)

Water was not clean in Elizabethan England, so Jack and Angus would not have looked out of place drinking beer or ale.

Did people really climb up the Colleges in Cambridge? (p.88)

When Jack and Angus found themselves on top of the spires of King's College Chapel, they were partaking in the old and dangerous tradition of free climbing on the roofs, colleges and chapels of Cambridge. Students and fellows of Cambridge have since indulged in many other activities and pranks; in 1958, Cambridge awoke to see an Austin Seven motor car perched on the roof of the seventy-foot-high Senate House.

Day of Deliverance

What was the Armada Campaign and what led to it? (p.46 onwards)
Following a period of unrest between England and Spain, the Armada
Campaign began when a large Spanish fleet set sail to attack England
in 1588. The conflict first started when Philip II of Spain came to the
defence of his Roman Catholic religion, believing that Protestant
Elizabeth I was a heretic and an illegitimate ruler of England.
Elizabeth supported Protestant interests elsewhere in Europe –
particularly in the Netherlands, where she encouraged a Protestant
Dutch revolt against the Spanish who ruled there. Philip supported
the various plots to overthrow Elizabeth, and her execution of Mary,
Queen of Scots only strengthened his desire to defeat England.

**What did the Spanish hope to achieve during the Armada
Campaign, and what actually happened?**
Led by Duke of Medina Sidonia, the Spanish had planned to make
their way up the English Channel and rendezvous near Calais. With
an experienced army in tow, the Spanish hoped to cross the English
Channel in barges and make their invasion of England.

The outcome, however, was very different. The Spanish fleet set off
with about twenty warships, one hundred merchant vessels, and
about thirty thousand soldiers and sailors. Sailing up the English
Channel, they created a defensive crescent with their fleet, pushing
back the English line of around two hundred ships. The Armada
made good ground very quickly, anchoring their ships off Calais. As
the Spanish waited for orders, the English launched an attack, causing
panic; many of the Armada fleet had to cut their anchors. The
following day, England and Spain met at the naval battle of
Gravelines. Five Spanish ships were lost and the remainder headed
north up the east coast of England. By this point, many of the Spanish
ships were badly damaged. After this, the fleet was caught up in a
series of storms around the north and west of the British Isles.

Around twenty-six of the Armada's ships were wrecked off the coast
of Ireland, another off the coast of England and two more off the coast

of Scotland. Just two ships remained relatively unharmed. Around two-thirds of the Spanish army died – for every one killed in battle a further six to eight were executed, drowned or died of thirst, hunger and disease. Furthermore, many Spanish wrecks were plundered by locals and the survivors were robbed and murdered. In comparison, English losses were minimal, but even after the victory, disease and hunger killed many English sailors and troops.

Why did the Armada Campaign fail?
There were many reasons why the Armada failed:

Poor leadership, planning and communication between Philip II and his leaders. In contrast, the English fleet was headed by seamen with great experience.

Tactics and technology. The Spanish preference, and traditional naval fighting technique, was to use the ship as a platform to grapple or ram the opposing ships, which they would then board. In contrast, the English used guns to attack the opposition without boarding. English guns were more accurate, had a longer range and were fired many times more often than the equivalent Spanish guns. Moreover, in the years leading up to the Armada Campaign, English ships had been significantly redesigned by John Hawkins and the first master shipwright, Matthew Baker. They were 'race' (meaning 'razed') built – longer in the keel, which meant that they sat lower in the water. This made them faster and more manoeuvreable. In the thirty years of naval warfare during this period, no English ship was sunk by Spanish gunnery.

Home advantage. The English fought in waters they knew well and the Spanish ships, when wrecked, found themselves in hostile countries.

The weather. As the Armada retreated from the naval battle of Gravelines, the Spanish still posed a significant threat. However, as many of the fleet were badly damaged and the Spanish army were suffering from injury, disease and shortage of provisions, they were poorly prepared to survive the storms that awaited them as they made their way back to Spain.

What happened after the Armada Campaign?

After its defeat, the Spanish navy was reformed and managed to keep control of its home waters and ocean routes well into the next century. In England, the legend of Elizabeth and the Protestant cause lasted for years. Some believed that God was behind the Protestants during the Armada Campaign, and war medals were printed bearing the inscription 'He blew with His winds, and they were scattered'.

Was the naval battle of Gravelines a turning point? (p.170)

The Armada's attack at Gravelines was just one major event in a succession of conflicts during the Anglo-Spanish wars that occurred between 1585 and 1604. In reality, Gravelines was not as significant as portrayed in *Day of Deliverance*, but the defeat of the Armada certainly boosted England's confidence and naval power.

Who was William Shakespeare? (p.19)

William Shakespeare was an English poet and playwright, and is regarded as the greatest writer and playwright in the English language. Born in 1564, Shakespeare wrote thirty-eight plays, one hundred and fifty-four sonnets and several poems before his death in 1616. His plays have been performed more often than those of any other playwright.

Who was Christopher Marlowe?(p.25)

Christopher Marlowe was an English playwright who attended King's School, Canterbury, and Corpus Christi College, Cambridge, on a scholarship. There has been speculation that Marlowe was a secret agent working for Sir Francis Walsingham. Marlowe's work includes *Dido, Queen of Carthage, Tamburlaine, The Jew of Malta* and *The Tragical History of Doctor Faustus*. Although he does not carry the prestige of Shakespeare, his plays were very successful. It is thought that Marlowe may have been assassinated. His only portrait hangs at